To my wife Latrice Johnson,
Without you, a better me would not exist.
I love you!

PROLOGUE

Present Day

I t was another cool and wet May night in Newark as Speechless Moore walked the dark backstreets of Jersey's Brick City. He caressed the concealed Dead Air Wolfman silencer connected to his nine-millimeter. As he had done in his last ten missions, he kept it tucked inside a compression waist strap pressed tightly to his body.

The possum that scurried across his path had made more noise than he had. Everything about him was silence personified. His all-black attire gave him the appearance of a shadow. His high-grade boots were custom made as tough as combat boots but as quiet as ballerina slippers. His solid-colored wool hat boasted no distinguishing labels or marks. His reputation for keeping quiet attributed as much to his nickname as had the way he left the few witnesses that he'd purposefully allowed to walk away. Tonight, no one would be that lucky.

Speechless didn't care if the target was male or female. Didn't matter if they were black or white. The only color that mattered to him was green. Money green. He didn't care how they looked, or about the loved ones his victims would leave behind once he stripped them of their existence. He'd done this many times and was immune to any emotion tied to murder. He was good at exterminating people for hire, among other things. There was no way to sugarcoat it. He killed people for a living.

Tonight, his contract was a prominent City Councilman. The murder of city officials became high profile-cases with lots of media attention. Attention he would make sure never led back to him under any circumstance.

As he approached the target's home, he began to feel that familiar surge of excitement that had always consumed him. It enhanced his focus producing a personal rage towards his victims as if they had personally violated him. It was the driving force that made him so successful at both elimination and liberation of guilt.

As he patiently waited in the hedges, his massive stature kneeling in between the luxurious homes in the plush section of Newark, he thought about the path that led him to this life. His youth in particular when he'd been arrested. He considered the day he was sentenced to four years in juvy for aggravated assault, his new birthday. That day Kelvin Moore died, and Speechless was born.

From that day forward, he was all about reaching the next level in whatever he did. His self-confidence and caliber of self-worth were attributed to years of reading, studying, and perfecting himself. He used his time wisely, absorbing information as if he were a human sponge. He stored useful knowledge he could apply later on in life as the situation occurred, or the opportunity presented itself.

As he grew with each passing day inside the adolescent prison, he became smarter in more ways than one. Quickly he learned that not everything worth knowing could be learned from a book. He developed the knack of association and connection. His affiliation with dudes like Wise, The Professor, and Too Smart, may he rest in peace, proved useful and vital. Over the years he'd built a list of loyal friends, partners, and soldiers. Some he trusted with his life. Only one he trusted with this part of his life.

Speechless shut off the euphoric recall of his younger days, and the loss of a comrade and snapped back to the mission. Once it was safe to proceed, he approached the estate his target occupied. He readied himself by popping a peppermint into his mouth which he'd hold in the left side of his cheek until the job was done.

With ninja-like stealth and professional ability, he crossed the yard and sneaked behind the house, and used a miniature pair of wire cutters to disable the alarm system that was connected to the house and adjacent three-car garage. After disabling the alarm, Speechless then extracted a pair of diamond-tipped glass cutters from his waist pouch. His mentor, Salvatore, had gifted them to him. As he had been taught, he cut a small hole into one of the windowpanes on the backdoor of the home. Within seconds, he was inside, his alert eyes scanning every inch in front of him and around him: the kitchen, the ceiling, the walls, and the stairs that led into the oversized basement. Speechless drew his firearm and followed the sound of voices. He ascended the carpeted stairs into the double-wide hallway that connected the south wing of the house.

Then, he saw them. Word in the underground was that the bald city councilman and his aide, Maxine, were both heavy into child pornography, as well as child trafficking. Speechless shook his head in disgust as they both sat on an imported Persian carpet in front of what appeared to be an eighty-inch flat screen HD television, their hands intertwined and fingers playfully massaging each other, watching the movie *Sleepers*.

Without hesitation, he spoke one word. "Hey." He didn't need to yell. The bass in his voice was carried and demanded attention. Startled, the two sadistic lovers turned toward him. Speechless shot them each twice with his silenced pistol. Crimson pools of blood formed around each sprawled body, dying the plush off-white carpet a deep, dark red.

With shocked expressions on their faces, their bodies sprawled on the floor twisting in agony. Struggling in vain, they could not stop the blood seeping from their neck and facial wounds. Not out of pity or compassion, but simply because he needed to see the job finished with his own eyes, Speechless walked up to them shooting them both in the head and watching their bodies go limp.

Slipping out of the estate, Speechless drove to an abandoned housing project in Orange to burn the evidence of his latest job. Once he parked in the rear of the abandoned projects, he exited the car then climbed five flights of stairs until he came to an empty apartment that contained only a large steel trash bin. He put on a pair of throwaway gloves and reached behind the trash bin until he found the small container of kerosene. After he doused the bag and the inside of the bin, he lit a wick made from twisted old newspaper and set the bin ablaze. Once the fire got going, he removed the gloves and tossed them into the flames before he lit up a blunt of sour and smoked it until the entire bag of evidence was burned to nothing but ashes.

On his ride home, he thought about the young, tight pussy that was awaiting him. Of all the women Speechless bedded, Tamara had been his favorite. She was young, ambitious, and extremely attractive. She came from money and carried herself with class and sophistication. Her Jamaican father's portfolio of ventures included a successful chain of laundromats, dry cleaners, and real estate in and around Newark and East Orange. Her Italian mother came from old money and was the daughter of a wealthy wine importer. Tamara was always well taken care of and didn't want for anything in life except love. Money couldn't buy love or loyalty. No matter how much of it you possessed.

Speechless had taken to calling her Tammy and he'd come close to making her a keeper. At just twenty-four years old with no children and studying in the field of Child Psychology to earn her degree as a Clinical Psychologist, who she was, was what made her that much more attractive to him. She was special, but then again, so were all the women he chose to fuck at his leisure. He was particular with the women he chose to spend time with, in any manner. The average woman didn't interest him.

He possessed qualities that were irresistible to women. His well-kept wavy hair, inherited from his Indian mother, constantly had women fawning over it just to run their hands over it. Three years of braces and retainers helped perfect his bright smile. But what most women fell for was his personality. He was a natural charmer, and his game was so smooth it rivaled a romance novelist. He didn't need to say much to be heard. Women couldn't resist his overwhelmingly confident swagger. Confidence was attractive and he had it in spades.

After stripping down from his assassins' attire, Speechless stashed his weapon and his tools in his secret hiding place. While he showered, he chewed his peppermint, allowing it and the steaming hot water to clear his nostrils and his head. Twenty minutes of shower therapy later, he stood in front of the seven-foot-tall mirror and oiled himself with baby oil, lotion, and cologne combination that he became addicted to while incarcerated liking the way the oil-blend settled into his skin and resonated long after it was applied. Once he applied pomade to his wavy hair and tied it down with a doo-rag, he dressed skipping a wife-beater preferring the defined appearance of his physique without one.

He completed his ensemble, with a fresh-out-the-box pair of Timberlands, his diamond chain, bracelet, and pinky ring. Fully dressed now, he gave himself a once-over in the mirror, strapped on his custom-made holster and ice pick to his calf, and headed for the garage. He contemplated taking the Mercedes S600 sedan but opted for the forest-green Range Rover HSE instead. Tammy loved the way he had coordinated it with green-tinted windows and matching twenty-two-inch floater rims.

Speechless preferred the Range whenever he had company in the car. The state-of-the-art sound system played music filling the silence because he didn't talk much. Cruising through the back streets of Orange, New Jersey, his wheels appeared to be still as the truck navigated the curves and corners, maneuvering further and further from his hide-a-way to the affluent suburb of Bloomfield.

Tammy stood in front of the antique mirror and admired the golden yellow push-up bra, panties, and matching sheer teddy that her man was sure to love. She stepped into some sexy heels and sprayed Flowerbomb by Viktor & Rolf all over her body. Speech had bought her a bottle for her birthday. His taste was expensive and exquisite, and she'd only ever wore the scent for him.

Her naturally long hair cascaded over her small shoulders, and she pushed it back letting it flow behind her. She'd laughed when Speech told her that she could've easily been a model. He constantly complimented her small frame and five-foot-nine height.

But Tammy liked the challenge of getting ahead in life using her brainpower. Not that there was anything wrong with being a model. In fact, in all honesty, any labor on her part was unnecessary. A career was simply something she chose to do. Her mother had been instrumental in getting her the bank manager position that she held as a mere pastime that afforded her extra income, as well as a platform to make connections. Her parents were well-off, and took very good care of their only child, spoiling her with the very best of anything she needed or desired. She drove the latest model BMW 325i Convertible, courtesy of Mommy, and her lease at the lavish condominium apartment building by her father, who adored his little girl.

After she received her Bachelor's in Finance, her mom and dad deposited one hundred grand into her savings account as a congratulatory gift. The trust fund they had created for her was currently valued at two-hundred and fifty grand. What would be willed to her if they passed would keep her set for life.

Her best friends, Tiffany and Brenda, both came from wealth as well. Together, all they did was shop, go out to eat, and party like there was no tomorrow. Tammy needed more than that to fulfill her life. She supplemented her life with work, Grad School, and of course, Speechless.

As she studied her reflection, her plump round ass, caramel complexion, and how it was all connected to long sexy legs that tapered off with wonderful calves, her thoughts were interrupted by the sound of Speech unlocking the front door to her place. They had been seeing each other exclusively for about four years now. After two years into the relationship, she had offered him the keys to her place, hoping he would move in, but he stated that he was far too independent to live with a woman under her roof.

As soon as he entered the condo, her pussy got wet. Once the scent of his cologne connected with her senses, her freaky side kicked in as she greeted him.

"Hey, Daddy. What took you so damn long? I've been waiting forever for you to come stretch this pussy out." She approached him and reached for his zipper. She slowly squatted in front of him and undid his belt, pulled down his jeans and boxer briefs in one fluid motion, before she started sucking his dick with the skills of a seasoned porn star. As she deep throated his manhood and sucked gently on his balls, Speechless played in her silky hair, massaging the back of her neck and top of her shoulders, caressing her with those ever so strong hands she adored.

He began to fuck her mouth vigorously and that turned her on more. She couldn't get enough of his long, thick, love pole in her mouth. She'd suck him off anytime and anywhere. They had fucked so many times, so many ways, in so many different locations that sex with Speech was never boring. He pleased her in so many ways and never seemed to run out of energy, even during their marathon sessions. They'd turn off the phones and hibernate for the weekend with no distractions from anyone, just enjoying one another's mind, body, and juices.

After she'd drained his dick, and swallowed every drop of his cum, she looked up at him with seductive eyes, licking her lips. "Now take those fucking clothes off and fuck me."

Tamara walked into the oversized bedroom switching her plump ass and slim waist in lace French-cut panties. She knew they were Speechless' favorites. But it was the clicking of her heels that enticed him most. She knew how to bring her man to an immediate erection again.

Stripping down completely, taking his time as she always suggested he do from the very beginning of their union, she watched him take his clothes off. Once he was done peeling off his clothes,

Speechless slowly planted soft, wet kisses from the top of her feet to her thighs, driving her wild.

Tamara craved to have him inside her but didn't want the foreplay to end. Speech lifted her legs onto his shoulders until her high-heeled feet were touching his shoulders and began to spread the soft flesh of her pussy lips with his thumbs, exhaling on her exposed clitoris, teasing it with his warm breath before he tasted her. As his tongue and lips touched her clit, she began to cum almost immediately, quivering under his oral pleasure, willingly trapped and wrapped in his massive arms.

She convulsed and writhed in ecstasy until she orgasmed multiple times. She loved this part of their lovemaking because she had responded the same way for the last four years. They switched positions, and she laid on her stomach, her perfectly round ass in the air giving him the access that he needed. Slowly, he entered her pulsating pussy from the back teasing her and pulling out of her repeatedly. By the third time of his teasing, she begged for him to penetrate her love box, only to have him pull out entirely and rub the head of his huge dick against her pulsating clit and lips. She couldn't stand it anymore and with all of her defenses collapsing, she screamed out passionately.

"Fuck me Speech! I want your dick inside of me!"

He slid in her womb and after a couple of strokes, she soaked his balls with her cum, spraying and squirting uncontrollably. Tossing her hair from side to side as he handled her ass and hips, she climaxed back-to-back. Sweat dripped from Speech's nose and chin landing on her ass and slipping in between her cheeks. Her lower back glistened glistening as he emptied himself into her, pouring everything he had into her being, draining himself completely.

After he'd fucked her thoroughly, they were on their way to the Italian Restaurant, La Villa Sicily, when Tammy mentioned wanting to upgrade to a Bentley GT convertible and asked Speech what he thought about the idea.

"I'm gonna have to get you an around-the-clock bodyguard if you get that car baby. Honestly, you don't need to be driving a vehicle like that through the streets of Brick City. It's dangerous." Good girls didn't know how ugly the ghetto streets were. Speech loved that she had that untarnished mentality but sometimes it was a chore trying to save her from herself. He turned up the radio a little essentially ending the conversation.

She didn't bring it up again and he appreciated that she valued his judgment. During dinner, Speech hadn't talked at all except to ask her how her food was and to address the waiter. She ate quietly and looked lost in thought. He usually didn't mind the silence, but not at the expense of animosity.

"You ok, baby?" He asked setting his linen napkin down on the table.

Tammy met his eyes and offered him a sweet smile before she nodded. "Yes. I was just thinking about the first time we met and our very first date. It seems like forever ago but at the same time, like it was just yesterday."

Speech lifted her dainty hand to his lips and kissed it. He wondered what prompted her to go back to that particular day, but he didn't ask. After he'd dropped her off at home, he couldn't get it out of his head. He laid in his bed, an arm behind his head as he stared at the ceiling. The day he'd met Tammy was a day he'd never forget.

ONE

A MAN NAMED SPEECHLESS

Four Years Earlier

SPEECHLESS

As soon as Speechless Moore eyed a rival boss entering the multiplex cinema with his wife and children, he turned to members of his 50/50 Crew, Rilla and Pretty Boy, and gave an order.

"You see Duke, right?"

Rilla casually nodded in response.

"Handle that muthafucka' and iron out those wrinkles."

Rilla nodded again before he disappeared.

With business out of the way, Speechless bought two bottles of water from the concession stand and focused on more entertaining prospects. He'd wanted to see the newly released movie but the young lady standing a few feet away with her two friends shocked him with her beauty and suddenly he'd preferred to watch her. She resembled the actress, Stacy Dash, who'd starred in *Mo' Money!*

Speechless and Pretty Boy walked over to where the young ladies were standing cool, calm, and confident. As he approached the trio of young females, he displayed a brilliant smile of all even and pearly white teeth. When they'd made eye contact, the beauty that had stolen his full attention began to blush.

"Hello, Miss." He addressed the beauty first and then her friends. "Ladies." His baritone voice could have easily belonged to the bass of a quartet singing group. "Excuse me. May I please get your autograph? If you don't mind?"

The Caucasian female with all the voluptuous features of a Latino woman began to laugh before turning to the third young woman among them. "Autograph? He's joking, right? Shouldn't we be getting his autograph?" She turned to Speechless with a flirty gaze. "What team do you play for?"

He'd been asked that more times than he'd care to admit, but the NBA hadn't been his calling despite his six-foot frame and large hands. Speechless, respectfully ignored the friend that had tried too hard and kept his gaze on the beauty that had caught his eye. "Since you're a movie star, I thought that I would take it upon myself to come over and get your autograph. And possibly give you my telephone number with hopes that you would call me as soon as your movie ended. If you aren't spoken for, that is."

The beauty smiled up at him amused. "I don't know who you thought I was, but my name is Tamara. And these are my friends Tiffany and Brenda. And since you're the movie star slash Mr. NBA, let me say that it's nice to meet you." Tamara extended her pretty manicured hand toward him.

Speechless gently took her hand swallowing it in his before he lifted it to his lips, planting a very soft kiss on it. "My pleasure."

TAMARA

She'd always told herself that she would rather drink motor oil than give some street thug the time of day, but the way that fine man approached her and how he carried himself, had caught her off guard. Not at all what she'd expected when she and her two good friends went to the multiplex movie theater in the Ironbound section of Newark. She'd thrown caution to the wind and set out on an adventure. At least an adventure for good girls who came from the suburbs. Newark was the ghetto and not somewhere her parents would approve of her hanging out. But she was turning twenty-one years old in a few weeks, and she needed to experience new things. New places. And apparently new people.

TWO
A PRETTY LADY & A PRETTY BOY

TAMMY

After the movie, Tammy had called Speechless, and they had decided to meet up in the parking lot of the theater. The Newark Police Department and ambulances were everywhere outside. It was rumored that one of the patrons had found a man dead with his face in the toilet bowl. As she walked to her car, she heard chatter that the victim had been stabbed in the temple. Someone else said he'd been stabbed in the throat. Everyone agreed it was murder.

When she'd finally found Speechless among the chaos, he didn't seem to care much about all that had been going on and instead asked the ladies if they were down to go hang out. After talking it over with her girlfriends, she and Tiffany agreed to go while Brenda had chosen to go home.

She refused to be the third wheel after one of Speechless's friends had said his goodbyes and departed in a hurry. When Speechless pulled up next to her BMW in a red Mercedes Benz coupe, she was shocked. She hadn't expected to see such an extravagant car in a Newark theater parking lot. She wasn't a big car enthusiast, but she couldn't help but admit that his ride was sexy. A deep red paint job, mirrored-tinted windows, shiny rims, and a little chrome trimming screamed seduction. She would bet her life there wasn't another car detailed like it in the entire world.

His friend, Pretty Boy pulled up in a royal blue Range Rover HSE, overly decked out. Where Speech's Mercedes was sexy and subtle, his was loud and obnoxious. And when he rolled down his windows it looked like a scene from a Cheech and Chong movie, there was so much smoke. Barely able to contain her approval of his whip, Tiffany subtly tapped Tammy on her back, when he pulled up. Tammy wasn't surprised. Tiffany had always gravitated toward loud, bright, and out-of-the-ordinary fashion, people, scenes, and life.

Speechless, had the girls follow him and Pretty Boy to a nearby twenty-four-hour parking garage, so they could leave Tammy's car there and not worry about it falling victim to the auto-theft epidemic that plagued Newark for so many decades. When they reached the garage, he pulled a wad of cash and handed the attendant a few bills for the occupancy and then turned around and gave him one more to make sure he took extra good care of this particular BMW convertible. By the look of the attendant's eyes, it was clear that Speech had tipped him well.

It wasn't even ten o'clock and they decided to eat at the Red Lobster nearby. Pretty Boy invited Tiffany to ride with him promising her loud weed. Tammy was hesitant but Tiffany was grown and before she could say anything he had already gotten in his car. At first sight, she had said she was feeling his swag and long-ass hair. Tammy couldn't say she was surprised when Tiffany didn't think twice about accepting his offer.

Speech eyed her before he motioned to his car with a flirty smile. They rode there quietly, and she didn't know what to make of it but just enjoyed his side profile. He was fucking sexy. He didn't need to say a word.

At the restaurant, everybody ordered and got familiar with each other. Tammy kept admiring Speechless in the light, and the way his waves, eyes, and diamonds glistened in the soft lighting. He damn sure looked like a pro Basketball player. When the food arrived, Pretty Boy and Tiffany were tearing shit up, with no shame nor restraint. Just shoveling food, no doubt the effects of being high off weed.

Tammy and Speechless laughed and smiled while they ate, amused at their friends and how the ice was broken between the two of them. It was weird how'd quickly those two had clicked. It eased Tammy's apprehension.

Tammy took notice of everything Speech did and said. She could see right away that he wasn't a careless man. He was deliberate in everything he did and said. A man of self-control and self-care. While everyone had ordered, steak and lobster, Speechless enjoyed his steamed salmon with white rice and a large plate of mussels and broccoli.

After dinner was done, they chatted a little. When Speechless opted to not have dessert, she declined as well. Tiffany and Pretty Boy had begun to feast more on each other and skipped dessert as well.

"Would you ladies like to go to Atlantic City with us?"

"Yeah. Blackjack's calling my name," Pretty Boy chimed in before he whispered something in Tiffany's ear that made her blush and giggle.

"I've been to Las Vegas, but never been to Atlantic City," Tammy replied.

"How can you two be from Jersey, and have never been to Atlantic City?" He seemed disappointed in her. She shrugged her shoulders. In truth, why visit AC when Vegas was clearly nicer, but she kept her bougie comment to herself. She was smitten with Speech and wherever he wanted to take her, she'd go.

"We kidnapping y'all tonight. Right Speech? Tonight, we gamble, and party until breakfast. That cool with y'all?" Pretty Boy chucked Tiffany under her chin and winked at her. She practically melted on the spot. Tammy gaged Speech's reaction. He nodded once in response to Pretty Boy but didn't say anything else beyond that. She didn't know what to make of that until he held the door open for her leaving the restaurant and tucked her hand in the crook of his elbow as they walked to his car.

Just like that, she was a passenger in his car as they rode down the Parkway. Speech had turned on some Sade and before they were halfway there Tammy had fallen asleep.

Speechless hit the last stretch to AC doing about ninety mph. He'd paid a nice price for the most advanced police scanners and detectors in existence, and it had been well worth the investment. He wasn't worried about getting tickets for speeding.

PRETTY BOY

Pretty Boy, on the other hand, was getting his dick sucked for the third time since he and Tiffany had left the parking lot of Red Lobster. When Speechless sped up and began flying down the Parkway, he kept to the speed limit. He was riding dirty with mad bud and a pistol. No matter what, Pretty Boy was always strapped!

Tiffany was pretty as hell. He couldn't help but trying to watch her suck his dick and drive at the same time. It took some serious skill, but he got it done time and time again during the long ride. It between cock sucks he smoked his blunts, passing it back and forth to Tiffany.

The bitch was one boujie and freaky female. She swallowed nut after nut. During one blowjob he had to put the car on cruise control. He took his feet off the pedals while she milked him, to avoid accidentally accelerating or braking and he loved it. Unlike his wife at home, Tiffany made serious eye contact while she was putting the dick away, and that shit turned Pretty Boy on like a motherfucka'.

THREE
HIGH STAKES GAMBLE

SPEECHLESS

As soon as they entered Atlantic City, Speechless waited for his partner on the first floor of the Taj Mahal Casino parking garage. He got out, walked away a few feet, and smoked a Dutch. He never smoked while driving because he always carried a weapon or two. Salvatore had insisted he did so. While he waited for Pretty Boy, he checked in on Rilla, Chinky, and Shorty Slice to see what was good, or wasn't, in the hood.

Smoking his blunt of kush, he discreetly chatted with his partners to get specifics as to what was going on with the various businesses they ran together. As he conversed, he looked back and saw Tammy rousing from her trip to la-la land. Speechless hung up the phone both pleased and upset at the updates from his partners. He was several hours away and there really wasn't anything he could do about it at the moment, except offer advice and make suggestions. For now, he'd focus on what was in front of him. Tammy.

Damn, she was beautiful. Even when slept. By the time that half of the blunt was gone as was his attention to anything else but her. Pretty Boy and Tiffany pulled up sounding like a club on wheels, as Tammy got out of the car.

He approached her keeping his virility in check. "Hey, Sleeping Beauty. We aren't parking here, so you can stay in the car if you want to."

Tammy winced before stretching a bit. "I have to stretch my legs Speech."

Speech? She couldn't have surprised him more had she called him by his birth name, Kelvin. He had only allowed one person to call him Speech: his half-brother Tito, Salvatore's only son. Yet, the way it rolled off her tongue so melodically she was banned from calling him anything but from now on. Damn, everything about this woman was sexy.

"Do you mind? We have been riding forever. Besides, I want to check in on Tiffany before we go into the casino."

Speechless brought the blunt to his mouth and dragged. He nodded his consent as he blew out. She could ask him to walk to the Boardwalk and back and he probably would've considered it. He laughed to himself. Nah. He'd never let any woman have that type of influence over him. Not in this lifetime anyway. But Tammy could definitely make him take some risks.

TIFFANY

Tammy and Tiffany went off to the side anxious for girl talk. Each spilled details about how they were feelin' Speechless and Pretty Boy and how they planned on letting them get the goodies. Tiffany admitted that she had already given Pretty Boy a taste on the way down to Atlantic City and that she was looking forward to putting it on him later.

"Girl, he is packing. I can't wait to see what that feels like up in me." Tiffany finger-combed her long weaved ponytail.

Tammy laughed. "I fell asleep in the car. Give me a mint. I left my purse in the car and I don't want Speech to see me pop one."

Tiffany cracked up as she pulled some mints from her purse and handed them to Tammy. "You fell asleep? Bitch, are you crazy? You need to enjoy that man's company. Do you see his car? He must be loaded."

Tammy popped a mint and handed Tiffany back the tin. "He's gorgeous and his car is sexy, but it's something about him that I like that has nothing to do with his car or good looks."

"Yeah. What's in his pants. I guarantee you that he's packing."

Tammy winked. "That's what I'm banking on."

Tiffany laughed and looked over at Pretty Boy. He was smoking the last of the blunt they were sharing. He gestured with his head for her to come back over to him and her stomach did a flip flop with anticipation.

"We'll talk more tomorrow. I'm going to go enjoy my night." Tammy nodded and headed back off to Speechless's car. Tiffany sauntered over to Pretty Boy like a jungle cat. He bit his bottom lip as he watched her walk over to him. Yeah. She definitely couldn't wait to give Pretty Boy some real good kitty cat.

TAMMY

When they entered Donald Trump's Taj Mahal casino, the women were in awe. They hadn't expected the opulence of a Las Vegas casino could also be found right in their home state. The purples and lavenders complimented with gold accents spoke depicted the grandeur Mr. Trump set out to create, in his one-of-a-kind casino. The carpeting was plush. The numerous chandeliers were humongous and rumored to cost more than two-hundred and fifty thousand dollars each.

Tammy suddenly looped her arm into Speech's' massive bicep and snuggled closer as they strolled around, taking in all there was to see. Tiffany and Pretty Boy were holding hands as if they had been dating for years. Tammy looked back at them, making funny faces at Tiffany teasing her for falling in lust so quickly as if she wasn't head over heels for Speechless herself.

They hit the blackjack tables first. Tammy and Speechless sat down to play. He pulled out a large amount of cash and handed Tammy a grand. She wasn't moved by that amount of money. That was petty cash to her, but she was a little surprised Speech had given her money at all.

He expected her to gamble his money? She graciously accepted it and kept her eyes on him. She wasn't a big blackjack player, but she was determined to have fun no matter what.

SPEECHLESS

Little did Tammy know, Pretty Boy and Speechless were damn near experts at playing the game. Both had played for years during their juvenile bids in the Southern New Jersey youth correctional system and spent hours mastering counting cards. They knew when to bet big or bet moderately. After two hours at the Blackjack table, Speechless was up eight thousand dollars and Pretty Boy, eleven. They were both smart gamblers, so they never stayed at one table too long. A trained dealer would eventually pick up on their hustle. Tammy was in awe of how well he played.

He collected his winnings and sat her at the Blackjack table, then stood behind her. He'd whisper in her ear when to tap and when to hold. Several times he remained quiet, and she knew he was testing her to see if she'd learned anything from the tips he'd whispered in her ear. She lost the first round. In the second round, he softly kissed her neck and it lit her within. She won several rounds after that. She heard him chuckle behind her and it pleased her that she had impressed.

After Pretty Boy lost a hand, he got up from the table and motioned toward the other side of the room. Tammy collected her winnings and laughed with Tiffany about how much she had won. Speech and Pretty Boy planned on heading to the Texas Hold 'Em Poker room sectioned off from the main gambling floor.

Speechless turned to Tammy, his voice smooth and sexy. "Do you know how to play Poker?"

Tammy shook her head and smiled. "Why? Do you want to teach me?"

Speech gave her a half-smile and chucked her under her chin. "One day Beautiful. How about you play the slots?"

She hid the blush that wanted to surface and kept her cool. "That's fine. Tiffany and I can hit the machines."

Speech leaned in and whispered in her ear. "Take those diamond earrings off and slip them in your purse, ok? Don't want anybody to try anything stupid. And be careful with your winnings."

Tammy nodded and did as he suggested. Speech slipped another grand in her hand and told her to have fun. "We'll be back in a bit."

Tammy bit her lip and smiled at Speech. He didn't have to do anything but look her in her eyes and she felt the chemistry ignite. "You too," she said.

After he winked at her, she turned and saw Pretty Boy handing Tiffany some money. She shoved it in her purse before she and Pretty Boy began kissing. He groped her ass as if they were all alone instead of in the middle of a crowded casino. He pulled away from her and smacked her booty before catching up to Speech.

Tammy watched Speech walking away, his swag setting him apart from every man in the room and from every man she'd ever met before him. She smiled and set off to the quarter slot machines to add to her winnings.

SPEECHLESS

At the poker table, Speechless and Pretty Boy never went against each other in a pot, unless both felt they really had the superior hand. In those instances, they had come up with subtle gestures to signal to each other. Wiping the corners of their mouths with index and thumbs was code to fold. If one of them bit his bottom lip like LL, that was the signal he was bluffing and getting ready to muscle this pot. Smoothing down their waves three times meant his hand was winning worthy. Over the years they'd change or moderate their silent signals. And over the years they'd won big money.

Tonight, they each brought in for five grand, and within two and a half hours had quadrupled their money to twenty-plus thousand dollars, generously giving the dealer and waitress fifty-dollar tips as if they were dollars. Speechless remained sober and drank only cranberry juice. As custom, they left the poker room to ward off suspicion. They found Tammy and Tiffany and escorted them to the Craps table, showing the beautiful ladies off and letting them blow on their dice. Sometimes They even let the ladies throw the dice for them. After winning big at craps, they headed toward the Roulette wheel. Pretty Boy asked the women if they wanted to get some breakfast before or after the roulette wheel, and they agreed to do it after.

"I don't want to break your lucky streak," Tiffany said, and Tammy nodded in agreement. Speechless looked at Tammy and nodded, not saying a word but glad she'd agreed. An unselfish woman was hard to find.

After Speechless lost some money at Roulette and Pretty Boy broke even, they called it a night. They went to a favorite local spot that stayed open twenty-four hours. Speechless listened as everyone ordered heavy breakfast meals with steaks, pancakes, home fries, and eggs. He ordered scrambled eggs with cheese, two bowls of hominy grits without butter, and two orders of dry wheat toast. He added his usual glass of cranberry juice along but added orange juice too. Now and then he liked to mix the two juices. When the waitress returned with the drinks and the extra glass of ice Speech had requested, he prepared his mixed drink as Tammy studied him intently. He pretended not to notice. When people didn't know you were aware of them, they tended to let the guard down and show you who they truly are.

Once breakfast was over, while the girls waited in the hotel lobby, Speechless had retrieved another weapon from his vehicle and after concealing his gun, Pretty Boy grabbed some Kush and Dutch Masters cigars from the center console of his truck.

The group headed to the complimentary suites that were offered to them while they were playing at the craps table. With the long night they had just had, they couldn't wait to relax, kick back, and unwind. Pretty Boy had arranged for neighboring rooms as a security measure.

They weren't in North Jersey but that didn't mean trouble hadn't followed them. Or they could have even been watched in the casino, especially after winning big.

The suites had been as lavish as the lobby and Tammy made her approval known as much as her desire. Once Speech latched the door lock, it didn't take much conversation to get Tammy out of her clothes. He could tell she was dying to take a shower and fuck him. Speech sat on the edge of the bed and just watched her move. She had this swag about her. She knew she was bad, but she wasn't conceited. Quiet confidence. She didn't have to try. That shit was ingrained in her.

When she took her clothes off without Speech even having to provoke or ask, he liked her all the more. She wasn't afraid to go after what she wanted. Speechless could not believe how fine she was, and decided on the spot, in his mind, that he was going to make her his unofficial wifey. He had numerous bitches, of course. He was a boss and women came with the reputation and lifestyle. He was one of the most sought-after hustlers in all of Newark. But Tammy wasn't aware of that, and that fact alone made him want to claim her because she wasn't in the streets, or from the hood.

Her matching peach push-up bra and lace French-cut panties did her scrumptious body wonders and made her look even more perfect than she did when she was fully dressed. His dick began to bulge in his pants at the sight of her.

She sashayed to the bathroom and looked back at him seductively. "Are you coming to take a shower with me, before I get in the Jacuzzi handsome?"

Without saying a word, he slowly undressed, allowing her the pleasure of taking in his well-toned physique. By the time he was down to just his boxer briefs and socks, she walked away, and he watched her ass and incredible calves disappear into the bathroom.

She was already in the shower once he entered the bathroom. He stepped into the shower and closed the glass door. Speechless didn't waste any time and approached her from behind, brushing her wet hair towards the front of her body and placing warm, hungry kisses all over the back of her neck and shoulders. As he sucked and kissed on her, he methodically moved his strong hands down to her juicy ass and began squeezing it, rubbing it, and caressing it with added lubrication from the body wash. When he saw how she reacted to his hands on her ass, he moved his hands up and around to the front of her.

He began rubbing, and softly pinching her hardened nipples, squeezing them between his ring and index fingers, and massaging them with his palms. Slowly he started kissing down, lowering himself to his knees, his tongue teasing the lower part of her back and top of her ass.

He nudged her inner thighs wanting her to spread her legs as wide as she could, and she immediately obliged him. He spread her butt cheeks and stuck his long tongue deep into her warm inviting pussy. As she arched her back and pushed her ass in his face, he gripped her hips and ass and stabbed her tight juicy pussy expertly with his tongue until she had cum twice in his mouth.

Tammy bent at the waist a little and he took full advantage of her position. He rubbed his dick up against her clit as he stood up, slowly allowing himself to slide back and forth between her swollen pussy lips. When she gasped as his dick head brushed her ass hole, he plunged his hard dick deep into her dripping pussy.

TAMMY

It was as if her sexual soul had been pierced, and the floodgates of emotions opened up flooding her core because she came like never before. Speechless gripped her slim waist and hammered her love box over and over, deeper and deeper and she didn't want him to ever stop. When they got out of the shower, they dried each other off and started the water in the Jacuzzi.

Tammy dropped a pillow on the floor and knelt on it before Speech. His dick twitched with anxiety. She began sucking his dick as if she were trying to earn a ring the next day. She squeezed him with both hands and sucked on the head of his dick. He tried to push her head away, but she knocked it away let him squirt his sperm, splashing the back of her throat.

He moaned as he ran his fingers through her hair and gripped her head fucked her mouth so she could swallow every drop of him. He put it on her, until the hot water in the Jacuzzi turned cold, and introduced her to numerous sexual positions she didn't even know existed. He fucked her until she was dehydrated and, reaching for the cold champagne, taking greedy sips at the glass once she grabbed it from him.

They drained the Jacuzzi halfway, refilled it with steaming hot water. Once the water was ready, Speech helped her into the hot tub before he got in and sat with his back against the wall, his arms around her. Encased and surrounded by mirrors and reflection, the sexual experience was even more erotic and passionate to her, as she allowed herself to get fucked in five different positions while in the water. She was beyond impressed with his performance and was damn near in love with him already.

Pretty Boy

Meanwhile, Pretty Boy and Tiffany were having an exotic experience of their own. Tiffany was a certified freak for anal sex and did not deny him the opportunity to explore every love port of her freaky body. They went through KY as if were lotion, both finding themselves with equal sexual appetites, and uninhibited imagination. They got more than familiar with each other in their unbelievably plush suite. Pretty Boy, like, like his comrade, had decided to make Tiffany his little wifey, on the side. The way she took his dick; from the back, on top, whichever way she would allow, she was like a porn star in training or something. Looking at her, one would never have suspected she was a freak on that level. The way she had his big dick in her ass and moved the way she did, was complete freak shit. Throughout their sexual escapades, they smoked four blunts and ordered room service.

Before everyone knew it, it was eight in the evening and the foursome had decided against going back in the casino to risk anything they had already walked away with. The women were more than satisfied with their winnings and had accepted their invitation to a trip to Cancun in a few months. The fellas, on the other hand, their winnings were nothing to hype them. They'd done it dozens of times. What was valuable to them was that they got the broads, caught a nice lick, but most importantly, they had a legit alibi.

FOUR
IT'S BUSINESS AND PERSONAL

SPEECHLESS

B ack home, after dropping the girls off at Tammy's car, Speechless and Pretty Boy changed clothes and regrouped. All hell had broken loose in Duke's controlled territory of Newark since his demise. Rival bosses were plotting to seize and conquer among the chaos.

Big Slim, Speechless's most eminent adversary, controlled most of the entire Ivy Hill area within the Vailsburg section of Newark. It was a decent size territory for one man to be the head over. For the past eighteen months, he and Speechless had warred over the fifteen-block radius that served as the home of Ivy Hill Apartments; a certified gold mine.

In that time, Big Slim had been responsible for the deaths of four of the 50/50 Crew's soldiers. All four died gruesome and painful deaths. Crazy Pete from Alexander Street was knocked unconscious then burned alive inside his car. Crooked-Nose Cory from Melrose was stabbed sixteen times then left alive in a garage with three vicious pit bulls that had been starved for several days. Within a week they had almost consumed his body entirely. Rico, from South Orange Avenue, was jumped after leaving a club in Downtown Newark. One person threw bleach in his eyes, and while he fought to see in front of him, someone came up from behind him and slit his throat from ear to ear. Last was Lil' Trouble. They did him dirty by tying him to a tree in Ivy

Hill Park and shooting him 14 times with a Tech-9. Twenty shell casings were recovered by Newark police.

Speechless was pissed by the assassinations of his comrades, but the death of Lil' Trouble enraged him. He was only seventeen years old and had been under the wing of the 50/50 Crew for the last two years. But even worse was that he was the baby cousin of Patricia, a Newark Police Officer in the fifth district and Speechless' main girl. Patricia was so upset by the death of her baby cousin, that she cursed anyone responsible for his savage and untimely death. Speechless knew that if Patricia had ever found out that Lil' Trouble had been hustling under Speechless, she would have left him and never forgiven him. But more importantly, she would have had him arrested.

RILLA

After he killed Big Slim at the movie theater, Rilla had to finish what was started. Timing was essential in taking over all of Big Slim's territory. Word hadn't gotten around yet that Big Slim was dead so his whole organization was business as usual with their guards down. As soon as he showered and changed clothes, Rilla was on the phone with Chinky and Shorty Slice, to let them know that the storm cloud had cleared up; code for 'Our enemy is dead. Time to take over.'

Each of the 50/50 Crew partners, minus Speechless and Pretty Boy, mounted their all-black, bulletproof Lincoln Navigators, accompanied by five soldiers. They were armed with AK47s and Mac 10 machine guns. Some carried a few revolvers, and everybody wore their vest.

8They strategized and split up, each fully loaded war vehicle heading toward different sections of Vailsburg. The plan was to simultaneously target every area of Big Slim's territory and taking out as many key players as possible to leave little room for retaliation. They lived by the mantra that if everyone was dead, there was no one left to retaliate

Big Slim, had three trusted captains in his organization. Twins, Terry, and Jerry Mitchell had grown up with him and were his closest and most trusted partners. Freddie, known as Freddie Floss, because he was always flexing, stunting, or flashing on somebody somewhere, was the third captain and had earned his spot-on top by once taking a bullet for Big Slim. His loyalty was well known and as were his whereabouts. Floss had always been cocky enough to think he was untouchable and was always out and about showboating. Rilla had never liked him. Then again, Rilla didn't like many people.

When his truck pulled up on Sanford and Mount Vernon, nobody knew what had happened at the movie theater down the hill, so they were all getting money and going about business as usual. Once they saw who had exited the truck, everybody got nervous. They all started speaking out of respect and apprehension. Rilla could see right through the phony shit and could sense their fear.

"What it do, Gorilla?" Rilla had no idea who that fool was.

"What's up, Gorilla? How you, Man?" The one standing beside him, Rilla did recognize but didn't know his name. His punk ass was just as shook.

Then came a face he knew all too well. "Yo, Gorilla. What's good? What brings you around these parts? I ain't seen you in years, duke." Freddie Floss lifted his chin and Rilla could tell he wasn't happy to see him. Floss was right to be on guard, but it was too late. When Rilla spotted Freddie, he hit the chirp alarm to the Navigator. Like SWAT on a mission, suddenly, the Navi doors burst open. Four shooters jumped out, spraying anybody with bullets standing in the immediate area just as Rilla reached into his waist, pulled out a 38 snub-nose, and shot Freddie in the face at point-blank range. As Floss's body fell backward into the bushes and concrete, Rilla emptied the hand cannon into his face and chest before he jumped back in the car and drove away, his mission complete.

SHORTY SLICE

The Mitchell Twins, Jerry and Terry, each ran their areas in Ivy Hill under Big Slim. Jerry, the older of the two, ran Mount Vernon Place, down the hill, near the stores, bank, and barbershop, while his younger brother by seventeen minutes, Terry, ran and controlled the projects in The Ivy Hill Apartments. It was Terry, who had discovered that Lil' Trouble was spying on their operation while pretending to romance a little cutie from the projects. It was also Terry that enjoyed watching him scream as bullet after bullet tore into his little body. Each member of the 50/50 Crew deeply felt the death of Lil' Trouble. He wasn't just a young comrade, but he was everybody's little brother and had one of the biggest hearts in the entire crew. He had been destined for more in life. Speechless took him under to protect him and hopefully one day see him do something bigger than run the streets of Newark. He owed it to Patricia to care for her family the best way he knew how.

After his death, everyone that loved Lil' Trouble, wanted to be the one personally responsible for the retaliation and make sure his murderer suffered a terrible fate twice as cruel. As the speeding black Lincoln Navigator headed up Mount Vernon it came to a screeching halt.

Romey had yelled for Petey to stop driving. "Yo! That's Terry's ride."

His burnt orange Mustang stood out like a sore thumb in these parts. Everybody knew it was Terry's car. Shorty Slice looked around and pointed out the window. "The motherfuckin' Twins are right there in the pizza parlor."

The opportunity to eliminate two birds with one stone wasn't a coincidence but fate. There was no way these pussies were going to make it out of that pizza joint alive. Petey cut off traffic and spun the Navigator around. Shorty Slice and his five-man unit were out of the truck before the driver could completely park. When the SUV came to a halt, Jerry already had his radar up and was taking his berretta off safety. Little did he know that his boss was dead, and he would surely join him sooner than he imagined.

Rushing across the street, weapons drawn, Jerry instantly pulled out his 9mm ordering his younger brother to get down behind the counter. As soon as Mills, Romey's cousin entered the pizza parlor, he was met by a bullet to the neck and another bullet shattered his collarbone. As he watched him go down, Shorty Slice could hear rapid loud gunfire coming from behind him, as his team let off a found heavy round of artillery in the direction of the shooter.

The echo of the gunfire in the pizzeria was so loud, that the patrons and proprietors in the liquor store next door could be heard screaming in fear. Bullet after bullet found its target, as the first one struck Jerry in his shooting hand, freeing the deadly seventeen-shot weapon from his grasp. Another bullet hit him in the face, just above his upper lip, splitting his mustache. Two more ripped through his chest causing him to go crashing into the table and chairs. A barrage of bullets made impact to his head, sending him into darkness forever.

Shorty Slice hopped the counter, his miniature .45 caliber in hand, and shot the store clerk, and Big Slim accomplice, twice in the face. He then turned his weapon on Terry who shot at Shorty Slice, catching him in the shoulder. Shorty Slice's adrenaline was rushing, and he reacted putting six subsequent bullets in Terry's body.

The two biggest members of the remaining soldiers, Shorty had with him, picked up the body of Jerry Mitchell, stuffed him in the massive pizza oven, and closed the door. Then, they turned around to his dead twin brother, and did the same, with the oven below the first. They'd burn on earth before they burned in hell.

CHINKY

As each faction of Big Slims' army was destroyed, Chinky was riding from block to block, spot to spot, spreading the word that Big Slim was no more and that the entire Ivy Hill section was now under the control of the 50/50 Crew. His offer to those that remained alive was simple.

"Be down, or be under? Your choice!"

Everybody in the streets knew what that meant. You either chose to be down and pledge allegiance to them or be under the dirt, pushing up daisies. Anybody that rebelled or dare mumble a smart remark was shot dead on the spot. Chinky did not play any fucking games and did not hesitate when it came time to kill enemies from rival drug crews. He didn't walk or drive the streets of Newark 'watching his back' because anybody he even thought posed a potential problem, whether present or possible in the future, was eliminated. None of them really watched their backs because the level of respect and fear they had earned from others in the town was unmatched.

The 50/50 Crew had put in so much work since the early days of their formation. They were notorious in Newark and had earned every ounce of the respect given. Every fallen comrade, or boss of a rival crew that died, was another step up on the ladder toward success. They now controlled eighty percent of the entire Vailsburg section of Newark, thirty percent of North Newark, and half of the Weequahic section. Part of the territory they controlled in the Weequahic section led into Irvington on one side and Hillside on the other. Naturally, whenever territories bordered there was always tension, Namely with the Butcher Boys that controlled Irvington and Hillside.

The Butcher Boys were backed by the Italians, and always had the best of the drugs, weapons, and protection. Their clique was known as 'mutts' in the hood because they were comprised of Jamaicans, Puerto Ricans, Indians, Blacks, and crazy-ass White boys that always felt they had something to prove.

The mob would never blatantly enter those neighborhoods. Instead, they started opening up shops, recruiting the Butcher Boys to run shit for them. Their business practice kept their pockets fat with street profits, and their hands clean of first-hand crime. Time and time again, the Butcher Boys would chop a motherfucker up just to stay fresh in the

Star Ledger, and in the minds of anyone that would test or oppose them. If a murder happened in Hillside or Irvington, the Butcher Boys were responsible, and the local newspaper reminded everyone of how gruesome and gory the murders were. A signature for the Butcher Boys.

SPEECHLESS

Meanwhile, up in Vailsburg, shit was chaotic, and everyone spread the word that the 50/50 Crew had taken over Big Slims' turf, leaving only a few alive but many dead in the process. The 50/50 Crew met up at the pool hall they owned, and kept clean, in the Weequahic section. The only exception of artillery was the shotgun behind the counter that the manager Smitty wouldn't hesitate to pull out and flash on anyone being disruptive in the spot. There were plenty of pool table arguments that were broken up by Smitty and his shotgun.

All of the 50/50 Crew partners were in attendance. Chinky and Shorty Slice were in charge of the Vailsburg section, which had recently been expanded tremendously due to the assassination of Big Slim and the seizing of his territory. Pretty Boy ran a very profitable thirty percent of North Newark with a population made up of eighty-five percent Latino. Speechless, along with Gorilla, ran the Weequahic section. Collectively, the territories netted them eight million dollars annually. The slower days were balanced out with the busier ones.

Now they could add three million dollars a year from Big Slims' former area. Of course, everyone wasn't content with just a million or so a year. Motherfucka had lavish lifestyles, expenses, and responsibilities. Hustlers at heart, they always thought of ways to expand and take over someone else's territory to strengthen the 50/50 Crew.

Nobody got money outside of the crew. No one except for Speechless. His murder for hire by the mob was lucrative as well as secretive. None of the 50/50 Crew partners knew of his side business. In all the world, only two people knew he was a contract killer. Salvatore, his mentor, and Patricia, his main. Patricia was legit law. A policewoman. But before she was a Beat Cop, she was a hood girl from the same streets that had raised Speechless.

Chinky, Pretty Boy, Gorilla, Shorty Slice, and the top boss, Speechless. They all were bosses and partners, but it was Speechless that sought out everyone individually and brought them into the fold. He was the top boss, no questions or jealousy about it. Everybody lived and fucked like kings.

Everybody in the crew made more than enough money, but they had something inside of each of them, that compelled him to desire more power and more wealth. The more people that feared them the richer they would be. Plus, they all shared a variety of legit businesses that pulled in an additional two million every year. They ran Newark. The grocery stores. The arcade. The taxi business. The bail-bondsmen. 50/50 Crew ran it and Speechless oversaw it all.

As the 50/50 Crew, sat around the card table playing poker, they discussed the latest accomplishments, and the inevitable outcome: war. Big Slim had connections, and he provided for a lot of local families, so naturally, those people affected by his death would be out for blood.

"Man, I don't give a fuck about none of them pussy ass niggas, because we are all that matters. 50/50 Crew for life. Anybody in our way is getting fucking stepped on," said Chinky.

"It's whatever with whoever. All you motherfuckers sitting at this table know how I feel about each of you. I would not hesitate to put a chump in the dirt for any of my brothers. Point. Blank. Period!" yelled Gorilla, who always got excited when shit jumped off. He was always the one to say 'Fuck it' whenever the crew couldn't decide on partial peace or war. Gorilla was numb when it came to the life or the feelings of anybody outside his crew. They were all he had for many years, and he would do and had done anything for the survival of his unit.

"Listen, what's done is fucking done. Next motherfuckin' phase is whatever it is, we move before they move. We kill everybody and anybody related to our motherfuckin' enemies." Speechless shuffled the deck of cards with ease of hand and tone. "If we think the Butcher Boys might get recruited for any parts of this war, then they ass is meatloaf too. What the fuck? We built this shit up from nothing. With nothing but our hearts and our gangsta. Every motherfucka that fell at our feet, every bullet sprayed, everybody that got tossed off the fucking rooftops, was for our team to be on top."

"You cats know where I stand. With all of you and your families. Anything for *mi familia*," said Pretty Boy. "Everything I have is 'cause of y'all and the hard work we put in. Ain't nobody fuckin' that up. Everybody dying. Real fuckin' talk."

Shorty Slice, the smallest and youngest boss in the 50/50 Crew didn't say shit. He didn't have to. He was just as gangsta and deadly as his big brothers, but like their leader Speechless, Shorty Slice didn't talk much. He did put that work in with that straight razor though. More times than many. He caught more jokers slipping than the police. At the car wash, the drive-in, the drive-thru. Shit, even at red lights, he caught cats banging their music and forgetting about drama. Dumb ass losers. Yet, Shorty Slice never got caught slipping because he listened twice as much as he talked, and he never put his back to a possible rival.

He was called Shorty Slice because he was only five feet six inches tall and weighed less than two hundred, but he was solid. He was stocky, because of his love for weightlifting, but he was fast as a motherfucka and loved to slash a niggas throat. His victims' reaction was both shock and desperation, which rendered them helpless blood squirting out of their necks.

Speechless dealt the cards looking each of the men in their faces as he spoke with conviction. "In the meantime, it's business as usual fellas. We flood the entire Ivy Hill with bigger and better shit. Tell all the captains that their workers are to be generous. Not cutting corners. Reward is guaranteed."

FIVE

HERSTORY & HISTORY

Two Years Ago

PATRICIA

B rought up in the Seventeenth Avenue Projects also known as the Hayes Homes and being raised by her father and uncles, of the locally notorious Blackwell Family, Patricia Vivian Blackwell was the biggest tomboy in her neighborhood growing up. Her mother had died of breast cancer when she was only six, and for years she wondered if her mom would ever reappear and walk through those doors again.

It wasn't until she was seventeen years old and had almost finished high school that discovered her beauty. The neighborhood drug dealers had always preyed on the high school upperclassmen, and she wasn't excluded. When they'd began to show her attention and harass her daily, that she realized she was attractive. Time and time again, people would comment on her looks. She never really paid it any attention because she was too wrapped up in the R.O.T.C., and her aspirations of joining the D.E.A. Immediately after graduation, she was in the police academy, and soon after that, she was on the fast track to making detective at the young age of twenty-five. She also had met and fallen in love with a handsome businessman named Kelvin Moore.

During her first year as a detective, Patricia had been partnered up with an asshole and loose cannon named Detective GG, short for Go Get'em, a nickname he'd earned for his radical tactics in apprehending those wanted. Too late had Patricia learned that he was the grimiest, most crooked cop on the entire force. GG had worked for the Canelli Crime Family and during his ten-year career as law enforcement had gotten away with over eighteen murders: some indirectly but most as the trigger man.

Back then, Detective Patricia Blackwell had been oblivious to the numerous illegal dealings that went on under her nose, so when the feds arrested and indicted her partner, she got caught up in a whirlwind of trouble. All her hard work tainted and collapsing at the hand of someone else. She had ridden an emotional rollercoaster so traumatizing it drove her to the brink of suicide during all the chaos. She didn't know why, but she was relieved when GG confessed to the many infractions and verified her innocence. There was still hope that she could achieve her government-level dreams.

Once back on the police force, Patricia became very anxious and aggressive. Despite GG's confession she had decided to downgrade from detective to patrolwoman and monitored the mini projects known as Bradley's Court.

As she walked the beat in Vailsburg she became familiar with the name and the notoriety the Canelli name carried from years and years of organized crime stories around Essex County. She was angry with the Canelli family for almost destroying her life.

One day while on duty, Patricia received a dispatch that a woman was being assaulted by her apparent boyfriend, at the gas station on South Orange Avenue and Munn Avenue intersections. The gas station was right around the corner from the Bradley's Court Houses, Patricia was able to get there within a minute. As she arrived, Joseph Canelli Jr., grandson of the Canelli mob boss, was screaming at the top of his voice at a battered and bruised brunette, whom she would later learn was Sylvia Calzonetti. Sylvia was the daughter of notorious mafia contract man and *Capo di Capi*, Salvatore Calzonetti. She was bleeding from her left eye and mouth. Joseph wore a pair of brass knuckles and before he could strike her again, Patricia drew her weapon.

"Freeze! Don't you dare put your fucking hands on her again! Get your hands up! Let me see them both up high!"

"Fuck you pig!" Yelled Joey Jr., as he put his hands high in the air. A crowd began to gather outside and in Valisburg Park, situated across the street from the incident.

Patricia approached cautiously and demanded Jospeh turn around and put his hands behind his back. He obliged but refused to do so quietly. "Do you know who the fuck I am, Cop? I'm Joey fucking Canelli Jr., and my family probably owns your boss, Bitch!"

"Shut your fucking mouth," she spoke nonchalantly and intentionally handcuffed him tighter than necessary. "Miss, are you going to be alright?" Patricia asked Sylvia. "The paramedics should be here any second now. Please have a seat in the police cruiser that has just pulled into the parking lot, and answer any of the officer's questions that you can. Ok, Ms.?"

As the officer exited his car to assist Sylvia, two more cruisers sped into the lot of the gas station and parked abruptly. After reading Joseph Canelli Jr. his Miranda rights, Patricia handed him over to one of her male co-workers, Officer Malik Smith. Officer Smith was a giant of a brother who'd been known to mad-handled men who beat on women. Malik roughly put Joseph in the back of the police car he was driving and when Joseph kept ranting and refusing to be placed in the cruiser, Malik slapped the hell out of the ranting mobster.

While Joey Jr. was being seated in the rear of the car, and Sylvia was being questioned, Patricia noticed Joey Jr. glaring at Sylvia, no doubt in warning to keep her mouth shut. It didn't work. Sylvia told Patricia that Joey had drugs and guns in the trunk of his Jaguar and that she would testify in court to whatever she had to. She cried and said she was tired of being beaten and threatened all the time.

Patricia followed up on Sylvia's intel and within an hour had stumbled upon the biggest bust of her young career. Not only did she find eight kilograms of pure heroin in his trunk, but she also recovered two submachine guns, four silencers, and a 357 long-nose revolver, which ballistics later proved was used in the murder of a federal witness four years prior.

After the arrest and arraignment of Joseph Canelli Jr., his grandfather, the Don, was infuriated and immediately ordered that the young female police officer responsible for ruining his grandsons' life, be murdered. He didn't even allow the contract to be ordered through his chief assassin Salvator. Instead, he reached out to Sicily personally and asked for the favor from his cousin, Isaac Canelli, also known as Isaac, The Icepick who promised to get it done.

For weeks, Patricia had the feeling that she was being followed, everywhere she went. She was never one to easily get scared, but this wasn't paranoia. This was a sign; a cautionary dissuasion as to what was truly going to occur if she didn't keep her guard up. She was no clairvoyant, but she paid very close attention to premonitions she experienced. Kelvin had expressed that he felt something was wrong too and told her to not worry. They'd get through whatever it was.

SPEECHLESS

Salvatore Calzonetti, met his longtime friend and pupil Speechless, at one of the most serene and safe locations they had chosen over the years they'd known one another, the beach of Atlantic City. As the old mobster walked around slowly picking up seashells, Speechless talked about everything from their first encounter, when he had saved Salvatore's life, to the current events of his love life and how he felt about Tammy, despite having Patricia. But knew he had to ask the only person that could have an answer to the very difficult question and his present worry involving his girl and the Canelli Crime Family.

"Salvatore, my dear and trusted friend, does the Canelli Family have a contract out on the policewoman responsible for the arrest of Joseph Canelli Jr.?" When Salvatore hesitated, Speechless had his answer but wouldn't just let it stop there. "Is there anything you can do to intervene? I know you and the old man go way back?"

"He is very distant and deeply hurt by the fact that not only his son but now his grandson will spend the rest of their lives behind a prison wall."

"So has he placed a bounty on her head?"

"Yes, my young friend, and he has not included me in this process of recruitment either. He has reached out to the old country. To a very close and dangerous relative that goes by the name of Icepick. Isaac "The Icepick" Canelli. He is an extremely deadly and accurate assassin. All of his contracts have been completed. He has been terminating for twenty long years, Son."

Speechless shook his head, not at all surprised by Sal's intel. It was what he expected. But that didn't change what needed to be done. "Can you get me any kind of information, or a description of any kind, on the hitman? It would mean a great deal to me."

Sal nodded his head thoughtfully. "I can do that for you, my trustworthy companion." He reached into the inside pocket of his jacket and pulled out an envelope handing it to Speechless. "You were going to get this package sooner or later. I believe this is also the one responsible for the disappearance of my sweet Sylvia."

Speechless couldn't keep his surprise to himself. He had always been careful to keep detached from his kills, but the sudden rage swelling up inside of him escaped. This motherfucka was contracted to kill his woman and was now possibly responsible for the disappearance of his sister? "He's responsible for Sylvia?"

Salvatore Calzonetti didn't answer the question but faced Speech sternly. "Just make sure that son of a bitch is dead."

After he left Atlantic City, Speechless studied the contents of the envelope Sal had handed him. Inside was a list of known aliases, along with in-depth details of disguises Icepick frequently used. On the long ride back to Newark he was able to process the information over in his mind and memorize the various photos of Icepick so that he could spot the right target.

It didn't take much effort to find Icepick Isaac. Everywhere Patricia went, no matter where she ventured, even at work, Speechless followed her. Not only for her safety but because he was certain Icepick was following her and he was right. For weeks, Icepick studied his target oblivious that he was being very closely followed and studied by her protector,   Speechless.

SIX

ICEPICK

PATRICIA

Patricia took her time picking out an outfit to wear. Tonight, her co-workers were taking her out to celebrate, for her once again becoming a detective. She pulled out the low-cut peach-colored dress from her closet that showed off her curvy figure and muscular legs. She would pair that with some peach sling-back heels made by Jimmy Choo, and the diamond necklace that Kelvin had given her on their second anniversary.

Looking at the time, she cursed that the time had slipped her by, and she'd be late if she didn't hurry. As she usually would, she set her gun atop the toilet seat before she stepped into the steaming shower. Taking a few minutes to allow the hot water to alleviate her tension and mental worries, she thought back to when she and her boyfriend Kelvin had met and fell in love so quickly.

Patricia was leaving the nail salon located in the same plaza as Out Fast, a bail bondsman and money-lending office when she noticed a tall, handsome brother walking out its doors before getting into a brand new silver BMW 750. She could see the definition of his muscular physique under his tailored suit and admired his wavy hair from a short distance. He caught her staring and exited his automobile to acknowledged her with the most handsome smile she had ever been graced with by a man. As he approached her, his air of confidence was a little intimidating and made her slightly nervous.

"Excuse me, Miss? I don't mean to bother you, but my name is Kelvin Moore and I had to come over and tell you that I am absolutely intrigued by your beauty." Speechless shook his head as if in shock.

"Pleasure to meet you, Mr. Martin. That is very sweet of you to say. My name is Patricia Blackwell."

"I assure you that the pleasure is entirely mine."

Patricia hid the blush that tried to emerge and kept her cool. *"Do you work at the bail bondsmen's office, Mr. Martin?"*

"Please call me Kelvin. And to answer your question, I own it business among others around town."

"Well, aren't you impressive?"

"I have worked very hard since I was young to obtain the many things I treasure. I am proud to be a very successful entrepreneur with several enterprises."

"Like that nice car you're driving? Do you treasure it as well?"

"Of course, I do, but it is in no comparison to the degree of appreciation I would have for a treasure such as yourself if you were mine," Speechless said to her.

Patricia smiled to herself at the memory. Speechless was unlike any man alive and she was grateful that he was hers. Her thoughts were abruptly interrupted by a sound and a shadow rapidly growing beyond the shower curtain! She panicked, and her breath caught in her throat for a few seconds.

"Who's there?" She asked trying to sound brave as she reached through the slit in the shower curtain toward her gun. Before she knew it, the intruder yanked her out of the shower by her wrist as she screamed out for help. The assailant wrapped his left hand almost completely around her mouth as he positioned himself to strangle her with the shower curtain.

Patricia frantically fought him in an attempt to get free, but his overpowering strength and her lack of oxygen proved to be too much as she found herself becoming numb. As she drifted into unconsciousness, a bigger shadow eclipsed her attacker, before blood splattered the tiled walls and floor.

Her boyfriend's voice could be heard through the haze and bewilderment. She must have been hallucinating from lack of oxygen and blood circulation. Kelvin was in Las Vegas working on an important business venture and couldn't be there. As her vision began to clear, she could not believe what she was seeing as Kelvin wrestled the invader before he slammed him across the bathroom sink, breaking it completely. Kelvin then picked him up again and threw him through the bathroom doorway into the foyer. With ferocious agility Patricia didn't even know Kelvin possessed, she watched him pound on her attacker.

Hungrily her eyes took in every detail of the scene before her. On Kelvin's left pant leg, she saw a holster strapped to his thigh. When he reached for it again, she knew what made the blood splatter across the bathroom. He was wielding an icepick that had to be at least nine inches long in her estimation despite him maneuvering it as if it were a pocketknife. Expertly, he moved and struck the man. One stab. Then another. Kelvin pivoted avoiding the attacker's counterattack before he stabbed him a third time.

Patricia could see the assailant didn't have a chance, his body moving slowly and clumsily now as blood poured from all over his body. She watched, speechless, not even attempting to go for her gun and apprehend the man who had unlawfully entered her home.

Patricia jumped as he mustered up some hidden energy reserve, pulled two similar-looking icepicks from his back, and began fighting blow for blow, swing for swing. It didn't last too long as he had lost a significant amount of blood. In the end, the killer lay dead, stabbed a total of twenty times. Kelvin had been punctured twice, but the wounds were superficial, and he refused to make a big deal about them.

The following few weeks brought up more questions than answers, but Patricia made sure the police report was concise. The investigation was open and closed quickly with her testimony and because she was attacked in her own home. Her fellow police officers and superiors allowed Patricia to recover and get back to her life. Her boyfriend, of course, was not charged in the death of one Isaac Canelli, a native of Palermo, Sicily, and distant relative to one Vito Canelli.

Patricia still had so many questions for Kelvin, and he sat her down one day and answered them. It was like being in a dream. Hell, it was more like being in a nightmare when Kelvin told her what he did for a living. He took her to the very genesis of his life as an assassin and relationship with Salvatore Calzonetti leaving her wishing she could wake up from it all.

SPEECHLESS

He knew one day he'd have to tell Patricia about this part of his life, but he didn't imagine it would be because someone tried to kill her. He told her about the day that changed his life when he saved Salvatore from being robbed and nearly beaten to death by six hoodlums from East Orange. He told her how Salvatore vowed to take him on as a pupil and teach him how to be a professional killer, and that he was forever in young Kelvin's debt. He told her about the many contracts he had carried out on various officials and selected targets, and how much money he made doing so.

Patricia sat there quietly staring at him in shock. He tried to wipe the look of fear that crossed her face as she pulled away trembling. Part of him wanted to console her but a bigger part needed her to snap out of it and channel the fighter and no-nonsense woman he knew her to be.

Speechless loved Patricia the best way he knew how, but more than love he needed her on his team, one hundred percent. Love was secondary to life, responsibilities, and being straight. Patricia had grown up to a hard life. She wasn't a soft woman. It was one of the reasons he chose her. It had all been planned. He knew this day would one day come and it was time to unfold the next part of his plan.

Speechless divulged vitally incriminating information because he trusted Patricia. He loved her unconditionally, and would do absolutely anything for her, but also because it was all part of the game.

One of Speechless' many talents was the art of manipulating people, especially women. First, there came the compliments and charm that always led to the bed. With each conquest, he'd cater to her every desire and give her unbelievable life-altering sex. When her emotions and body were peaking, he'd seal the deal by enrapturing her mind.

Conversations about the accolades, achievements, aspirations, for even greater heights they could gain together. He made women feel wanted but even more, so he made them feel needed. But it was all game. He knew Patricia was a cop even before they had formally met. It was precisely her career that he had singled her out. He needed to have a connection on the right side of the law. Someone to ensure 50/50's well-being and warn them of any surveillance or investigations.

Smart was an understatement. Speechless was highly intelligent and meticulous. He was a boss, and rightfully so. Even though he had confessed to being a hitman, he didn't reveal all of his secrets to Patricia. He still hadn't told her that he was the top boss of the reputed 50/50 Crew she had heard so many stories about. She knew what he needed her to know for the time being. He would not let her in on that secret for quite a while. First, he had to take their union a step further. So, with her eyes full of tears, Kelvin stood up, moved the chair to one side, and reached in his left pants pocket. He knew she'd never expected what he did next. Speechless lowered to one knee and opened the Tiffany jewelry box displaying the flawless, twelve-carat princess-cut diamond asking her to share the rest of her life with him. Patricia looked at him shocked but without hesitation nodded joyously, accepting his proposal.

SEVEN
BETRAYALS

One Year Ago

FRANKIE

For years, the Canelli Crime Family ruled most of Essex County including Bloomfield, Bellevue, and Montclair. There had been many battles over the turf, and many lives lost, but the Canelli family was triumphant in taking over and maintaining control of their territory. Even as other families from out-of-state attempted to profit or extort for a percentage of these prosperous cities and towns, they were met with extreme violence, and every other day there was a bloodbath in these areas. The newspaper was always covered with stories of the Canelli Crime Family and its cohorts, but there were never any severe repercussions or sanctions. Witnesses to prove any of the countless allegations were essentially nonexistent.

It was when they collectively tried to branch out into other places in Essex County: Caldwell, East Orange, North Newark, and South Orange, that the major problems began occurring with law enforcement agencies abroad. When powerful political figures began to be personally affected by the menace of the mafia, then those powerful individuals began to speak out against the mob, creating a revolving door of headaches and problems for everyone that were covered by the Canelli family umbrella.

Don Vito Canelli was the head of the family and the final decision-maker. His son Joseph Canelli Sr., slated to one day take over and run the family business, along with his ambitious young cowboy of a son, Joseph Canelli Jr. or "Lil' Joey" had both been convicted for a list of crimes a mile long, leaving Don Vito distraught and without an immediate heir on the outside. Yet he still had loyal underbosses he considered family. Beneath the boss in rank was underboss Frank Imperioletti, who had been friends with the Don for thirty years and had been instrumental in the rise of the Canelli Crime Family throughout the years. Then there was the *Capo di Capi*, Salvatore Calzonetti.

Calzonetti was chief executioner, first call with exclusive hits and necessary wet work because he'd proven to be the best and loved his work. Yet Salvatore was not the hitman for the Canelli Family.

Joe and Moe Gianello-Terazzo, who both could have played offensive linemen in the professional football league and were known as The GT Boys. Their mother, Verona Gianello, married their father Michael Terrazo when she was only seventeen years old but were then separated when he was slaughtered years a few years in a battle for power between families. The two brothers were her only children. They were three years apart in age but looked and dressed like twins their entire life due to the inseparable bond they shared and cherished.

The last Capo was Leonardo Zapada known by everyone as Mousy because of his small stature, high pitched voice, and weasel-like character. Mousy told and reported everything. He was the troublemaker, instigator, and got off on starting rumors. He was the distant cousin to Don Vito Canelli, so he was always pardoned for his lack of brutality and ability to lead. Yet he had been proved useful as a master in deception. Many times, he had organized and set up massacres masked as humble meetings or peace treaties designed to wipe out the heads of other families, their hierarchy, and muscle.

Like many times before Mousy had been up to his scheming and approached underboss Frank Imperioletti with a giant envelope, and a wide devious grin on his face. The contents of the envelope would change the entire structure of the Canelli Crime Family and created a permanent unbalance in the trust that was established many years ago. The carefully secured package, when it was opened by Frankie contained various mini-cassette tapes and photographs.

Within the large envelope were five white smaller envelopes. Two of those envelopes were marked with the name 'Salvatore,' and the other three envelopes marked 'Vito.' When he saw the name of his boss on the envelopes, Frankie's heart froze up, and his breath caught in his throat. He began to nervously look around and check his surroundings, even though he was completely alone. First, he turned his attention to the envelopes marked with Salvatore's name, as he tore them open one by one, he saw photographs of the hitman meeting with a big black guy. The more pictures he saw, the more he could see that the pictures were taken over a period of years. They both appeared to be younger in a few of the photos and older in others.

Next, Frankie began to look at photos of another familiar face, one he had only seen three or four times in the twenty years he had known Isaac "The Icepick" Canelli. There were pictures of him throughout the collection. Some of the pictures were different faces and characters, various masks of the same killer, and other pictures of The Icepick, had the black guy in the background, tailing, following, and watching him. He picked up the mini-cassette recorder and a cassette that was labeled Atlantic City. As he began to listen to it, he could hear a conversation despite the seagulls and wind in the background. *"Is this the man that they have recruited to kill my lady, Salvatore?"*

"Yes. They call him "The Icepick" because it's his weapon of choice, as he carefully conceals at least two to three of them on his person at all times. He is very ruthless, calculated, and smart my son. A very dangerous man not to be taken lightly in the least sense. You must kill him as quickly as you possibly can if you are to protect your precious Patricia."

Then it began to register with Frankie, that Officer Patricia Neal was the bitch police officer responsible for young Joey Jr. going to prison for life and exposing the Canelli Crime Family's involvement in areas beyond Bloomfield. He intensely listened as Salvatore continued.

"You must do this to protect her and also honor me, as he, the man within that envelope, I believe is the person responsible for the disappearance of my precious princess Sylvia, in retaliation for her testimony against Joseph Canelli Jr. at his trial."

Frankie cursed listening to the betrayal of their most skilled *Capo*. He tuned out the heartfelt talk about the little bitch Sylvia and focused on the meat of their conversation.

"Thank you so much, Salvatore. I know how much you risked to obtain such crucial information for me, and I know the consequences."

"When they decided to get rid of my daughter, they chose to betray me and become my enemy. All the years of loyalty from me. They could have pardoned her emotions for Christ's sake! He had been beating on her and terrorizing her since high school!"

"Don't you worry about Mr. Icepick. He is as good as dead. 'History books' as we say in the hood amongst my family."

"Also, within the confines of that envelope is your next target of elimination."

Upon hearing that last statement, Frank's level of curiosity began to increase, and he was confused once more. That was until he had heard the end of the tape.

"I have made a very lucrative living working for you all these years Salvatore. You have been a great mentor to me, and you're like the older uncle or stepfather I never had. Very influential in my life. Plus, you're the most generous man I know. You didn't have to share fifty percent of the business offered to you, but you did. I guess it's like you have been on vacation for four years, huh?"

"Don't think I was being so generous. I trained you as my young apprentice as a benefit to me as well as you. So indeed, I have been on a much-needed and deserved vacation."

Frank Imperioletti was stunned. When he moved on to the other pile of envelopes marked Vito, he reluctantly grabbed one, for if he was shocked at the latest revelations with the trusted Salvatore, he only could imagine what truth or astonishing disclosures were inside the packages. The first one he opened up had various pictures of the Don and his security detail, different times and locations were marked on the backs of these particular photos.

Then, what he saw next both made his heart sink and blood pressure rise simultaneously. He was looking at pictures of his lovely wife Mary Imperioletti and the Don Vito Canelli. Numerous photos, while they dined, walked hand in hand in parks, kissed, visited shopping plazas in other states, and her half-naked in the limo with Vito.

The pictures of her indiscretions were so numerous Frank started feeling light-headed and dizzy. His anger was raging out of control, and he had to sit before he passed or blanked out. It seemed like countless pictures of his wife and Vito having sex in out-of-state hotels and casinos from Las Vegas to Atlantic City to Niagara Falls, NY. Anna Marie was an avid gambler, apparently even with her marriage and loyalty.

Frank's mind went to work, and he thought back to all the times Mary said she was going to visit family in New York City, or when he himself was out of town on business for the Canelli family, or when the Don had to take extended trips to Sicily and would place him in command for months at a time. Then, he saw them. The pictures of his wife and Vito at his very own home, in his very own bedroom, engaging in sex. Tears ran down his cheeks and he balled up his fist tightly, as he internally vowed to ruin the Don, take over his empire, and kill his adulterous whore of a wife.

It didn't take Frankie long to figure that all of those photographs had to be taken by Mousy himself because there was absolutely no one who could gain that much access or such close proximity to the Don without being slaughtered. Now he just needed to know what the little weasel wanted in return for such vital information.

Eight
Legends Never Die

As he lay half-asleep in his customized king-size bed, Salvatore Calzonetti never imagined that his world would ever crumble. He had lived a channeled life of organized crime, and murder for hire. Responsible for as many as a hundred deaths during his gruesome career, he concluded six years ago to give it all up and sub-contract his orders to his secret apprentice Speechless.

Whatever contract Salvatore was hired for, he'd keep forty percent and Speechless would get sixty. A forty sixty split for hand over some information wasn't a bad way to make money in retirement. There was no doubt about it; the murder-for-hire business was lucrative and afforded any successful assassin a lifestyle some only dreamed of.

Throughout his career, Salvatore had traveled all over the world many times and had made and spent millions. Yet, he in his core was a sound businessman and loving father, and the nest egg of twenty-one million dollars that he had amassed was set aside for his only surviving kin once he left this world. Salvatore rarely spent his money in his older age. He lived moderately and secluded. Money was great but peace of mind is what he most desired along with leaving his family well taken care of.

His daughter Sylvia, his princess, was to inherit eleven million dollars. Tito, his son, who lived in another state altogether, was to inherit ten million plus Salvatore's most prized personal possession, his private journal.

Since the disappearance of his beloved daughter, his existence had not been the same. There was no meaning to his existence anymore leaving him feeling drained and depressed.

As he lay awake staring up at the vaulted ceiling, his thoughts were interrupted by a blur in his peripheral vision. He immediately went into defense mode and reached for the silenced pistol underneath the pillow beside him, once occupied by his now-deceased wife, Valerie. Valerie was gunned down ten years ago by a hail of bullets meant for him, in retaliation for the murders of the Petroli Crime Family's boss and underboss, that were at war with the rising Canelli Crime Family.

As Salvatore began to slowly rise from his bed, hand still gripping the silenced pistol underneath the pillow, a concussion grenade was thrown in his direction exploding and suddenly and loudly. Although the sound was deafening, Salvatore raised his weapon frantically shooting whatever and whoever invaded his immediate space.

Without his hearing, he couldn't pick up the sound of movement that he was usually in tune with. His ability to hear was just as important as his vision when it came to assassination and survival. He swung his firearm haphazardly unaware of which direction his enemy would attack. By the time he saw, it was too late. His left arm was severed at the elbow by a machete blade. Blood sprayed over the imported silk sheets. He yelled from pain, not from panic. He knew no one could hear him. He'd purposely chosen that house because of its seclusion and the distance from his neighbors. As he envisioned his life ending, he saw Mousy step from his place of concealment, grinning with his eyes, his mouth hidden behind the mask he wore. And he was not alone.

"Mousy, you weasel, son of a bitch. I curse you, and your fucking kids. You cocksucker!"

"Fuck you, you traitor," yelled Mousy in his high-pitched tone.

Before Salvatore could say another word, someone behind him stuffed his head in a thick, transparent plastic bag cutting off his air supply. The last thing Salvatore could see as he struggled to breathe were six men standing with Mousy, and each one armed with a machete.

SPEECHLESS

Hearing the news about his mentor Salvatore Calzonetti was devastating. His body had been scattered all around the Bloomfield, North Newark, and Montclair areas in ten different garbage bags; a mental image that Speechless could not get out of his head. He went on a warpath of retribution targeting the only people he could hold accountable for such a slaying— the ruthless Butcher Boys. One by one, he and his team sent body after body to the morgue. Seven of them in all, and the 50/50 Crew didn't ask any questions. They just knew that the Butcher Boys had violated, and it was very personal to their leader. Violating one was equivalent to violating all and wasn't tolerated on any level.

Just as Speechless expected, the killing of the Butcher Boys crew members didn't go unaddressed, and the 50/50 Crew had to bang it out almost every day with this wild bunch of hood desperados. Nobody was safe for months, and everyone had to extend their protection to the loved ones in their lives. When it came to war, real gangsters never played fair. There were no rules.

Pretty Boy's mom and Gorilla's aunt were each rushed and attacked coming out of a Bingo event hosted at a neighborhood church. Luckily, both women had only suffered bruises and lacerations, and no one had fired a gun at them. But they knew that it could've easily been much worse.

It was a very bloody year, and the drama naturally lingered. There was never a truce or peace established between the two rivals. The 50/50 Crew simply kept all operations away from Irvington and Hillside, and the Butcher Boys never stepped foot in any of the 50/50 Crew's territories.

Baby Hatchet

Hatchet had been the leader of the Butcher Boys for ten years, and when he was killed inside of a grocery store along with two of his workers, his gang was blind with revenge. His little brother, Baby Hatchet, pledged lifelong revenge. To make matters worse, he'd assumed the death of his brother would make him the successor, but he was wrong.

Chop, who was of Indian descent, took over and had been just as gangster as anyone around him. He was stepping into big shoes and just as Baby Hatchet always felt they had something to prove, Chop did too. One day, not long after he was inducted into the top position, Chop was invited by Baby Hatchet to roll with him and some dime pieces from Elizabeth. They were going to the Royal Benedict Motel ready to host a private party in the figure eight Jacuzzi's tubs the motel was known for. Couldn't get any better than good weed, good-looking broads, and family.

Chop had always been a sucker for ménage trios, and pussy was one of his few weaknesses and everybody in the crew knew it. Anywhere he went with a female that wasn't his main lady, the Butcher Boys sent a walking vest with him. Although he hated bodyguards, some extra muscle and hardware just in case some bullshit was going to jump off, or he was going to be possibly set up, had been necessary.

Baby Hatchet had shadowed his brother for years and because of that was extremely smart for his young age. He wanted power and had to make wise moves in order to put his plan into action discreetly. Neighborhood muscle was too risky to use. Instead, he enlisted the help of the Pocahontas Mamas, an elite female crew of rogue Indian dime pieces, who made their living off of setting up drug dealers who were either killed or blackmailed.

There were eight women in all, and they were the most beautiful hood bitches any man had ever seen. Each named after a jewel and treated as such by their sugar daddies. Five of them operated out of New Jersey, while the other three were down the bottom. Florida.

At the motel, Emerald, Diamond, and Sapphire were rolling up haze blunts and sipping on Moet Rose getting in the mood for a freaky time. Baby Hatchet had paid the girls ten grand each an unforgettable night of fun and surprises. He offered to pick up Chop so that they could roll together and leave together. Chop agreed.

When they arrived at the motel, the men could see the steam on the windows and smell the strong scent of weed wafting through the bottom of the door. When they walked into the room, Chop could not believe the beautiful Indian chicks awaiting him. Although he was Indian himself, he had not slept with many native beauties. These three were the most beautiful he'd ever seen, and that was saying a lot. He'd had a lot of pussy from all types of women from actresses, models, to strippers.

Emerald, the tallest of the women with red streaks in her long dark hair approached him, flashing her signature green contacts and perfect pearly smile. Without saying a word, she put a blunt in his mouth, pulled his pants down, and started sucking his dick. Sapphire came up from behind him, lifted his long blue-black ponytail, and started kissing the back of his neck.

Baby Hatchet was already in the Jacuzzi getting sucked by Diamond, watching Chop intently. As soon as Diamond drained him, he lit up a blunt and sent her over to join the action. Diamond approached Chop with a glass of Rosé and began sucking on his now exposed chest and nipples, blowing his mind, from the triple-action attention he was getting. He drank the champagne and tossed the glass somewhere in the corner with a muffled crash.

All three ladies worked on him until he started to sway a little, grabbing unto the ladies for stability. They maneuvered their way toward the bed, and gently pushed him back on the plush velvet comforter. Chop looked down smiling as two of them sucked on his dick and balls while the third was sucking and kissing all over his chest. Then all three of their heads were in his lap, sharing him.

The next day housekeeping skipped laundering the room because the Do Not Disturb sign hung on the doorknob. The following day, the maid on duty was aggravated that the sign still hung on the door past checkout time and was delaying her from completing her board. She knocked on the door but with no response. She pressed her ear to the door and still heard nothing but detected a faint odor. Annoyed she began to knock harder knowing she'd spend the rest of the day cleaning up vomit and a trashed room.

"Housekeeping! Are you checking out today? Do you need fresh linen?" No response. She repeated herself. "Housekeeping!"

When no one answered, she used her universal access key to enter the room. As soon as she opened the door, the pungent odor hit her like a slap from a heavyweight boxer bare-handed. She immediately covered her nose and mouth to block out the intense heavy copper odor, and the smell of death.

As she walked toward the bed, she noticed how clean the room was aside from the bed. It was messy and unmade, then she glanced up at the mirrored ceiling that was directly over the bed, and that's when she saw him. What at first, appeared to be the burgundy velvet comforter was a bedspread saturated in blood. When her eyes came in contact with Chops' body, she screamed so loud the front desk attendant heard her from a quarter-mile away.

The Coroner's office reported that Chop's wrists and throat had been slit. The most likely weapon was a scalpel due to the significant blood loss sustained from the clean-cut incisions. They also observed that the main artery on the right side of his pelvis had been lacerated as well, leading them to the conclusion that Chop had been unconscious before being wounded. The official cause of death was exsanguination. Chop bled to death.

NINE
RETRIBUTION

Present Day

SPEECHLESS

As Tammy and Speechless left the restaurant, she once again brought up wanting a new car. Frankly, Speechless didn't want any of his girls driving around the car-jacking capital of New Jersey in a three hundred-thousand-dollar car. It was too much of a temptation for stick-up kids. Tammy was easy bait even for the rookies of the game. Someone could easily take the car from her, then turn around and profit at least fifty thousand off the quick drop. Easy money.

"Why is it such a big deal Speech? She rolled her window down completely as she did whenever she was heated with him. You drive all kinds of exotic cars, and nobody messes with you. Don't you think that they would show me some respect being that I am with you?"

"That's not the point." Speechless pulled out of the parking lot keeping his eyes on the road. "Tammy, you can drive a Benz, Beamer, shit, you could even get a Jaguar if you want to baby, and please roll up that wind—"

Boom! Boom! Two blasts to his right side startled Speechless and he swerved before quickly recovering. The screeching of tires grabbed his attention and he saw a deep purple Escalade speed off ahead of him and caught a glimpse of something strange on the dashboard.

63

He looked to the passenger to check on Tammy and lost it. Half of her head was missing. Hair and brain fragments of his beautiful, ambitious, girlfriend splattered the dashboard and passenger side of the windshield, while the remainder dangled from her spine.

Speechless had killed enough people in his lifetime, in so many different ways, how he reacted to death differently. No tears. No emotions, other than anger and rage. He loved but to a limit. He would avenge her death because he cared about her but also because coming after the people, he cared about couldn't go unpunished.

Speechless quickly assessed the situation. Because she had not screamed out in pain or fear from the first blast, Speechless deduced that Tammy was dead from the first blast. He was grateful she didn't suffer and that her death was immediate although gruesome. Someone would pay fuckin' majorly for this.

Speechless immediately turned on the air conditioning to medium, before he flicked his high beam lights twice, pushed in the cigarette lighter, and stepped on the brake pedal simultaneously. A secret compartment in his Range Rover opened up displaying two chrome Beretta 9mm pistols, along with two extra clips and a box of ammunition.

Speechless sped off in hot pursuit of the Cadillac Escalade. He didn't get the license plate number, but how many deep purple Escalades were there in Newark? Racing through the streets, running red lights when there was the slightest pause in traffic, he spotted the truck near Springfield Avenue and High Street, two cars ahead of him at a red light.

When he reached for one of his guns, he saw blood and human fragments all over his right side. It was like adding lighter fluid to already hot burning coals. He sped around traffic enraged and opened fire on the rear windows of the purple SUV. Nine of the seventeen shots were dumped into the back of the Escalade shattering windows and puncturing the passenger door.

The driver took off zooming past the Society Hill section of downtown. Speechless was dead on his ass, doing at least eighty miles per hour. He aimed for the tires this time, shooting both back tires out causing the big, purple truck to slow down.

As he closed the distance between them, Speechless shot out the front passenger side tire. The Escalade swerved out of control, destroying a mailbox then hitting a telephone pole where it came to a halt. Speechless could hear sirens approaching, but he was blind with rage as he exited the Range Rover, the other Beretta in his hand. He quickly unloaded the gun at anything trying to move within the crashed truck and noticed that one of the dead guys in the backseat was a Butcher Boy. He was inked with a machete tattoo on his neck.

Speechless hurried to his truck and mashed on the gas as the reflections of police sirens bounced off the projects and neighborhood buildings, him barely getting away. He did not want to go anywhere near University Hospital, so he drove to East Orange General to report the incident and get treated for the buckshot in his shoulder and collarbone. He explained that someone tried to carjack him and Tammy on Park Avenue and Grove Streets, as they sat were parked. Tammy was shot as he pulled away from the curb trying to avoid the attackers.

STITCH

Meanwhile, on the Weequahic Side near Hillside, Stitch, a lieutenant in the Butcher Boys gang was talking to police and cooperating with detectives. His excuse for talking to the cops was to bring down the 50/50 Crew. But ratting was ratting, and snitches got dealt with. He was riding around in the backseat identifying members of the 50/50 crew. Those pointed out by Stitch were soon picked up hours later off the strip for petty crimes. He'd told detectives that one of the workers they busted in the organization would eventually roll over and give up someone big. But what Stitch didn't know was that every member of the 50/50 Crew was loyal until the death, under all circumstances.

Trying to sling dirt, he ended up under a pile of it. After one spiteful detective, upset that he had wasted his time, he leaked that it was indeed Stitch who was eating cheese. When word spread that Stitch was a snitch it was his fellow Butcher Boys looking for him everywhere and even sent soldiers to his known areas to shoot shit up. Others were deployed to the addressed of all of Stitch's bitches, and instructions were given to keep their fuckin mouths shut and call whenever he showed up. Cooperation and loyalty were purchased with the promise of a reward and not to kill them.

Butcher Boy soldiers went to his mothers' house on a rumor that he was secretly staying in the basement of her home, but when they attempted contact, she ignored their advances. They burned her house to the ground sending a clear message that they were not to be played with. She had been fortunate that she'd been out grocery shopping because they hadn't check to see if she was home or not. They didn't give a fuck about the loss of innocent life, and they were known for being ruthless and heartless.

Four days after the burning of his mothers' house, Stitch's rotting body was found completely covered with rats upon discovery. His dick had been cut off, stuffed in his mouth. He had been covered in melted peanut butter, left to be devoured by his own kind.

50/50 CREW

The war continued between the 50/50 Crew and the Butcher Boys, and many were slaughtered, caught slippin', and given a permanent dirt nap. Speechless took the deaths of his mentor, Salvatore, and Tammy very seriously. He declared the order to slaughter anyone, and everything involved with the fucking Butcher Boys.

"If you see a nigga at the fucking supermarket with the family, I don't give a fuck! Pop off and leave that motherfucka right where you see him if you got that strap on you. I don't care who gets hit, Nigga! Mask up, shades, and fitted, with the beard or the dreads!"

Because Speechless was a man of few words and little emotion, but whenever he spoke, he was taken seriously, and shit got done. Motherfuckas were getting hit at malls, car washes, movies theaters, in front of their jobs, parks walking their fucking dogs, and even their own homes.

Every single member of the 50/50 Crew was mandated to attend the shooting range regularly. What sense did it make pulling a pistol out, if you didn't have the good eyes or steady hand to hit your target or targets? Their diligence paid off. Wherever a Butcher Boy member was spotted, his death was on-site and guaranteed due to very accurate shooters.

In turn, members of the 50/50 had had their fair share of injuries and eliminations. Loved ones of the members were assaulted or shot at while living daily life. Innocent bystanders got hit by the hails of gunfire in a gang war that lasted over sixteen months. Nonstop, they went at it and created warzones wherever they went, or wherever the enemy was seen.

The Butcher Boys fought with vengeance believing the 50/50 Crew was responsible for Chop's death, just as Baby Hatchet had anticipated. The 50/50 Crew went relentless because the top dog said to be and they always prevailed, no matter what adversary or enemy they'd faced in the past.

Speechless was a great leader and provider of confidence to anyone with the slightest doubts. He was big bro and boss. He never let his team down or disappointed anyone in his organization. They thought that they were avenging the death of Tammy, his girlfriend and that was true, but they had no clue that they were also retaliating for the assassination of Salvatore Calzonetti. Two life ties to their leader. Still, when the fiancé of Shorty Slice was killed in an attempt to erase Shorty, the battle intensified heavily resulting in numerous fire bombings and kidnappings.

Ninja, a *capo* in the Butcher Boys, and his wife were snatched after a night out on the outskirts of Plainfield. They had been followed from their house in Hillside before being tortured mercilessly then killed. Their bodies had been strategically placed in the parking lot of Valley Fair for everyone to see.

His comrades and Jamaican relatives were angry beyond description, and they tried to turn it up by firebombing the arcade and grocery store owned by 50/50 in an attempt to catch one of the main leaders in the vicinity. Instead, they killed seven innocent kids at the arcade and three shoppers at the supermarket.

Immediately after, Speechless and 50/50 were already plotting and planning how they would flip and reinvest the insurance money for their damaged properties once those checks were cut including paying for the funeral expenses of the teens bombed in the arcade.

The streets ran bloody. Every injury or casualty suffered within the 50/50 Crew organization was returned five-fold to the Butcher Boys. Gorilla's girlfriend, Jamaica, was raped and beaten beyond recognition after she was kidnapped and left to die in an abandoned warehouse. She would not have survived the whole ordeal if it weren't for two wandering female crack heads found her. He was sure that had it been two male addicts, Jamaica would have been left to die. He rewarded the drug addicts with the choice of money or drugs, and when they told him drugs, he made sure that half a kilo of powder cocaine was delivered to the junkies in a vacant lot.

The courier was advised not to tamper with the package or deny the fiends their reward. He was to make sure they got whatever had been promised them. Gorilla would have given the druggies five bands each, but the drugs were cheaper to offer instead of the cash, so he was satisfied when they wanted white instead of green.

As Jamaica was protected and gradually nursed back to health at a private recovery center in Maryland, Gorilla spent as much time as he could by her side, keeping him away from Newark. His homeboys didn't mind his absence because they would have been granted the same liberty in a situation so personal. They all had mad love for her. She was down and as loyal as any 50/50 Crew member.

Everyone knew Jamaica and Gorilla had been together for six years and she was the Bonnie to his Clyde. Both being of Jamaican descent, they cliqued immediately when they met and went through a very emotionally intense beginning, almost causing him to leave the business.

He was forever loyal to his organization and would never abandon his brothers, but he was also madly in love with a woman he realized completed him, complimented him, and adored him. Most women were intimidated physically, or just attracted to the money he accumulated, but Jamaica accepted and appreciated him for just being Rilla. Those natural genuine qualities are what attracted him to her even more, and allowed him to let his guard down and let her in. He would spend the rest of his life making the men responsible for her abduction and rape pay, and they would pay with their lives.

At the funeral for Lil' Free, Shorty Slices' deceased fiancée, everyone was in low spirits. She was such a lovely young lady and they had had a very promising future. They had made such a good couple and were considered what some would call a perfect match. She was only five-foot-one inches tall and resembled the television hostess Free so much that everyone began calling her Lil Free as Shorty had nicknamed her.

Thet say a bullet doesn't have a name, and a bomb ain't got no aim but damn, some things just shouldn't happen. Lil' Free had been so beautiful inside and out, and it was a shame that her existence was cut so short by hood violence.

Immediately after her burial, when everyone was out celebrating her memory, Shorty Slice was out exacting vengeance on behalf of his soulmate. He cut deeply into throat after throat, assuring that each would no doubt bleed to death or be very lucky. Wherever he believed he would find Butcher Boy affiliate, Shorty was there. Dressed down with no-name brands or jewelry on, he looked like the average 15–year old kid in the hood.

Wee hours into the night Shorty Slice crept up on a rival when the rival's homeboy, who had come back after leaving, had called out to his boy alerting him to Shorty's advance. Surprised by the voice behind him, Shorty Slice turned around as three shots went off, one of which struck him high in the chest close to his shoulder. Out of panic, the two rivals fled the small confines of the Chinese restaurant, allowing Shorty Slice to get to safety, otherwise, he would have been slaughtered.

TEN
BURNING RAGE

SPEECHLESS

Speechless was focused on the ultimate revenge on those responsible for Salvatore's death, and he knew that no made figure could be assassinated without authorization from the Boss. In this case, the boss was reputed mob figure Vito Canelli. Speechless was well aware of the reputation and capabilities of the Don, but he didn't give a fuck. Somehow, someway, that motherfucka was going to pay for the murder and mutilation of his second father. He was still unsure how he would accomplish what he had to, to avenge Sal but he knew that he would come up with an answer soon. Strategizing had always been one of his strongest assets and why he had been so successful in running 50/50 and being Salvatore's protégé.

FRANKIE

Frankie Imperioletti was plotting his revenge against the two people in his life that ruined him emotionally: his wife Mary Imperioletti, and his boss Don Vito Canelli. No matter what the cost to him, their betrayal would cost them each their lives. Frankie was already a cold-hearted son-of-a-bitch, but when he learned about the affair that probably made him the laughingstock of everyone that had known, the little warmth he had left in him had been snuffed out like a candle on a windy night.

71

Frankie ruled his crew and *capos* viciously and his anger towards others reflected vehemently in the way he treated his cohorts. Anyone who was consistently late on payments or had begun to ruffle feathers was killed immediately. No questions asked and second-guessing. The root of possible trouble was dealt with. Frankie's tyranny had gotten ruthless to the point where it began to affect the Family's bottom line in certain areas. Money wasn't coming in as it once had. Many had been killed and the dead can't pay. The Don began to notice and weekly reports from Mousy had only confirmed what he had been suspicious of.

SPEECHLESS

What Speechless had going for him was that Salvatore had kept him in the loop when it came to the Canelli Family Organization. What Sal knew to get jobs done, Speechless would know too. Including, the fact that if anything negative came about between the 50/50 Crew and the Canelli Crime Family, it would be because Mousy had planted the seed. So first and foremost, Mousy had to be dealt with. Speechless spread a few dollars around here and there and had even given away a few bricks of top-grade dope to some fiends with very reliable information to find Mousy and kidnap him.

They looked around and patrolled the streets of Montclair, Bloomfield, and Bellville until they came across him at a bar shooting pool, along with his big mouth about how untouchable he was because of his affiliation with the Canelli Family. He yelled for the waitress to bring him another drink calling her a whore and demanding she hurry up. He was drunk beyond control. That had been his first mistake.

His second was doing so in a bar that had no affiliation with the family and therefore no loyalty to him or the Canelli's, so when Speechless slipped the bartender a very thick envelope to turn his head in the other direction, he whistled for the waitress and the two of them headed into the back and out of sight.

Before Mousy knew what hit him, Pretty Boy threw a burgundy pillowcase over his head and placed him in a sleeper hold until he was unconscious. Then he and his two henchmen carried him out the back door into the awaiting U-HAUL truck they brought and kept on reserve years ago.

MOUSY

When he regained consciousness, Mousy was still blindfolded and began to jolt and trembling in fear. His hands were tied above his head pressure on his wrists, as his legs flung below him, nothing for him to set his feet on. He was suspended in the air. He could smell the distinct odor of damp and mold and felt the cold air and knew he was being held in a cellar or basement. A baritone voice he didn't recognize came sounded close by and he figured he wasn't too far off the ground.

"How did the Don find out about Salvatore and the 50/50 Crew?"

"Who are you?" Mousy asked, his voice sounding pitiful in comparison.

"Who informed Don Canelli about Salvatore's relationship with my organization?" His abductor was furiously yelling now as he viciously wrapped duct tape around the mouth and nose of Mousy a few times so that he couldn't breathe. He felt like he was drowning before everything went black.

SPEECHLESS

Speechless watched as Mousy squirmed and struggled to breathe through the thick application of sticky tape. His complexion turned a deep bluish-purple and he had pissed his pants before Speechless cut a small slit into the duct tape, allowing him to take in air greedily and regain some faculties, as he was about to pass out.

"Why are you doing this to me? Do you know who I am connected to?" Mousy mumbled as he kicked and bucked back and forth in a futile attempt to shake free.

"Shut the fuck up bitch and stop all that moving before I have your feet removed motherfucka!" Speechless felt his rage overflowing but he had to show who was in control in this situation. "Bitch, you know what the fuck I'm talking about. Now explain this shit, or feel pain beyond comprehension, you cocksucker!"

Nearby Rilla turned on a tank and used the flicker of a welder's striker to light a torch. The flames whooshed free before a hiss echoed in the room. Speechless violently yanked Mousy's shoes and socks off spraining an ankle in the process. When the fire of the torch's menacing blue flame seared his Achilles heels one by one, Mousy's screams bounced off the walls and no doubt could be heard down the block. Unfortunately for him, no one lived within miles of their location and his screams for help were pointless.

As he choked on his saliva and screams, Speechless asked him again, yelling. "What did you tell the Don, and how did he find out about my family and Salvatore Calzonetti?"

"I secretly bugged all of Sal's suits." He paused panting before he started again in a rush. "And I followed the two of you to your location in Atlantic City. I took tons of photographs," Mousy whimpered. "I gave them to Frankie. He took it from there!"

Speechless gave the nod and without hesitation, Rilla swung a machete like a baseball bat. Both of Mousy's feet were cut clean. He screamed Again, the blinding hot heat came off the torch, as his ankles were burned into stumps. His hands and fingertips were scorched by the flame, bubbling and blistering his skin to the bone. He yelled out and shit his pants.

"Were you there when he was murdered? Answer me pussy!"

"No!" Mousy yelled, his voice muffled and pathetic.

"Liar!" Speechless yelled in a rage. "Pull his motherfuckin' pants off!" After his pants were pulled down in the front to expose his genitals, Speechless took the blindfold off and stare at the terrified Mousy. Then with all the cold-bloodedness of a vengeful son, he used the giant scissors to cut off Mousy's dick and balls Mousy looked down and saw his reproductive organs on the concrete floor before passing out.

After torturing Mousy for over two hours, they doused his body with gasoline and lit him on fire. He died screaming, repaying the motherfucka with the same torture he was sure his mentor had died.

ELEVEN
MASTER BLUEPRINTS

FRANKIE

Frank Imperioletti always ate at the same restaurant, his favorite restaurant, La' Italiano in Bloomfield. It was just the way he liked it and had always been this way. Italian-owned, Italian staffed, and only Italian-Americans served. Anyone else was either pressured politely to eat someplace else, or they were met with extremely bad service on purpose. As he sat with his mistress Bianca Lutzo, he enjoyed one of his favorite meals of braised lamb chops with linguini in red clam sauce, while Bianca nibbled on a salad and steamed mussels.

Neither of them was in love with the other and the relationship was one established out of convenience. She looked good on his arm, and he was good for her bank account. For years had been somewhat discreet about their affair, but since learning of the betrayal of his unfaithful wife and disrespectful boss, he no longer felt the need to show discretion.

He and Bianca ate side by side in a booth facing a mirrored wall. And as always, in between bites, he would caress her knees, thighs, and play in her delicious pussy. At twenty-four years old, she was half his age, but she didn't seem to care. He made sure she drove the best cars, ate the best food, and wore the best garments money could buy.

On the way home, Bianca sucked on Frank's dick while he drove and puffed on his cigar. They were so preoccupied they didn't realize they were being followed.

76

Speechless

A silver Mercedes disguised with matching silver-mirrored tinted windows, concealed four men: Speechless, Gorilla, Uzi Malik, and Shotgun Shawn. Uzi and Shotgun were both captains in the 50/50 Crew that had climbed up the ranks quickly. They loved the adrenaline rush of violence and had proven their loyalty over and over again.

Tonight, their mission was to grab Frank and his bitch inside his home, torture her to get to him, and then torture Frank to get to Don Canelli. Both men were giant like football players, their frequent trips to the County Jail the source of their massive build.

As Frankie turned down a quiet tree-lined street decorated with enormous homes and lush landscapes, Speechless noticed that Frankie began to slow down. No brake lights but he'd let up off of the accelerator. For the third time since they'd been on Frankie, Speechless could have sworn he'd seen a red Porsche Cayenne truck in his rearview. The first time was when he had pulled over to cushion his tail on Frankie. Then he saw it again as they crossed over into Caldwell, no doubt about it.

Suddenly, from both sides of the Cayenne truck came a barrage of automatic gunfire and muzzle flashes. The impact of bullets could be felt by those inside the Benz, but it was a useless attempt because the Mercedes was completely bulletproof. The consistent thumping and repetitious hammering of the slugs sounded like they had been caught in a rainstorm with hail pummeling all over the car.

When Speechless hit the gas and sped off, he watched as Frankie fled through the private gates of a secluded estate. Uzi Malik and Shotgun Shawn sat forward as Speechless hit a few buttons, exposing a sizable hidden compartment in between the backseat and the trunk. The backseat folded down and store within were brand new AR-15's and AK 47's equipped with night-vision scopes and infrared beams.

As the crew gripped up, Gorilla pulled up his floor mat and unlocked a compartment the size of a toolbox. Stashed inside were two .50 caliber Desert Eagle automatic pistols, professionally modified to shoot three substantial-sized bullets simultaneously with one pull of the trigger. One-shot from these monster hand cannons would undoubtedly remove a limb or an entire head.

Shawn and Malik were trained like every other 50/50 soldier that came up with a very specific strategy. Shoot for the tires, the engine block, and the windshield. Aim for the rear of the vehicle that way everyone in front and between would be slaughtered. Once there was a stutter in the attack on his Mercedes, Speechless knew some of the shooters were reloading their weapons and used the opportunity to counterattack.

"Now!" Speechless yelled to his team as the rear windows came down and the sunroof retracted. Without hesitation, all three men opened fire on the Porsche truck. Instantly, the trailing truck succumbed to the heavy automatic weaponry unleashed in a relentless hail of gunfire, obliterating the windshield, grill, hood, and tires.

When the Cayenne came to a halt, Speechless hit reverse and the 50/50 Crew kept on shooting tearing up the interior of the luxury truck and demolishing anything and anyone inside. The damage to the Porsche could have been mistaken for a fragment grenade exploding inside of it. The AR-15 and AK-47 assault weapons were way too powerful for the enemy and whatever methods of attack they used.

The echoing booms of gunfire resonated down the street as if it had been lit up like the Fourth of July. Motion sensor porch lights, garage lights, and car alarms were being set off, up and down the street. Lights began illuminating from within neighboring homes.

Gorilla stuck his hand and forearm out of the sunroof, aiming and firing at moving targets. Enemy after enemy, rival after rival, them niggas dropped. Driver. Passengers. Every single one of them.

Uzi Malik jumped out with the brand new AR-15 and let them motherfuckas have it up close and personal after their vehicle crashed and hit a tree. He dumped a clip on them bitches. Quickly he returned to the Benz, hopped in, and they were gone! They would come up with another plan soon after this fiasco died down a little. Their mission hadn't been completed. They would soon be back for Frank Imperioletti.

After Shorty Slice got out of the hospital, Gorilla's girl, Jamaica, was just getting out of rehab from the vicious attack, kidnapping, and rape during the war between the 50/50 Crew and the Butcher Boys. They had both suffered pain and trauma, but they were still alive and that was a reason to be happy. The 50/50 Crew had much to celebrate and to be grateful for. They rented out three floors at the Ravishing Hotel near the airport and hosted one of the biggest bashes of the year. Along with the releases of their loved ones from hospitals, they were celebrating inevitable victories, victories over the competition, over their enemies, and over the obstacles that had laid before them in the quest for supreme dominance in the streets of Newark, New Jersey.

That night, as the party raged on, Speechless found himself alone with Patricia in a suite bigger than their four-bedroom apartment, making passionate love to her. He wanted to soothe, console, and nurture her back to her confident self, assuring her that she had no more worries. Over and over again, orgasm after orgasm, he fucked her vigorously as if it were their first encounter; like he had something to prove.

Once the celebrating ceased, it was back to business as usual, and that meant war. Right from, Speechless ordered the mandatory killings of two Butcher Boy captains and three lower-ranking members. They got caught up at a house party that was just getting off the ground. All of the five ranking members were there, along with ten goons.

The horde of them moved about cocky and comfortable in their domain. Seemingly invincible. It was the kind of arrogance that pissed Speechless off. Soon enough, however, that changed. They didn't know what hit them as shooters from the 50/50 Crew gained access through bedroom and bathroom windows unexpectedly, opening fire on everyone, leaving no one breathing. They squeezed round after round at anything moving. Several females just hanging with their man or tagging along trying to get chosen, met the fate of being in the wrong place at the wrong time. They killed everyone, and every person trying to escape through the door got a shot to the head.

According to Patricia, the Newark Chief of Police was infuriated. He'd barked on anyone under him in rank or on his staff that dared opened their mouth to say anything. He was so damn pissed off he went as far as suspending anyone he didn't like or considered a slacker. He blamed the mass firings on budget cuts, spinning them as temporary lay-offs. He was upset about the frenzy of shootings and deaths piling up in Essex County, especially the most recent killings, where twenty people were murdered execution-style at an underground gambling house in his district, where three victims were young women. It had been the 'last straw' according to the Chief, and he vowed to Mayor Ribbons to rid the streets of Newark of gang violence and bring a cease to the senseless murders.

Speechless, contrary to what the police chief was talking about, was bent on painting the streets red with enemy blood and getting the necessary answers to the questions he asked. He was straight business, and anyone thinking shit was a fucking joke was a dead person. He didn't play games and wasn't about to start. He grew up ruthless and would remain ruthless because gangster was the only thing motherfuckas respected.

People didn't respect the old or the young, the black or the white. They didn't even have respect for religion. But gangster? Oh! Hell yes, they respected gangsters because they feared violence. Whenever gangsters were involved, you knew that something, somebody, somewhere was going to get hurt, or dead. Nobody wanted any parts of the end of the drama.

Speechless ordered four more hits and sat back while the bodies were collected, and the news reported. Losing two of the closest people in his life as a result of this war with the Butcher Boys didn't slow him down. He raged on and would avenge every ounce of their soul.

At the White Castle on Elizabeth Avenue bordering the Weequahic Section, four more Butcher Boy members were eliminated and two severely wounded when the 50/50 Crew opened fire on a crowd of them inside the parking lot. Shortly after a high-speed police chase ensued where a shootout with the assassins left one member of the 50/50 Crew dead, one captured, and three police officers killed on duty. Still, that didn't stop the war. Speechless wanted the top two men dead by any means. He offered up a two hundred- and fifty-thousand-dollar bonus for any crew member responsible for both deaths by the end of the Summer.

Everywhere either of the two leaders went, shooters were trying to get at them aiming to be the lucky recipient of that quarter million. The Butcher Boys were forced to recruit extra bodyguards and increase the level of already existing security. Still, the hunger of young wolves is a relentless one, capable of outrunning and outlasting anything or anyone. They don't stop once you are sniffed out and targeted.

Six weeks later, both Snake and Butch, the number two and number three heads of the Butcher Boys were found dead in Las Vegas inside an elevator. Surveillance cameras caught two hooded men whose faces were masked by bandanas assaulting the deceased repeatedly with icepicks in the face, neck, and head areas, before fleeing the scene.

In retaliation, Baby Hatchet sent goons to shoot shit up. They shot up corners, stores, and any blocks or territories controlled by the 50/50 Crew that they knew about. As a result, three soldiers and two workers were killed in the onslaught and unyielding assault. Of course, Speechless and the 50/50 Crew couldn't let that slide. They blew

Monique, Baby Hatchet's girlfriend's house in an attempt to kill him, but instead killed Monique, her two children, and her mother.

Kevin, her mother's boyfriend, who lived there at the time, was fortunate to be at work taking on an extra shift to bring more money home. Now, there was no home to bring money to. Baby Hatchet went underground after that. Buzz was he left the country. Others said he went southwest to Arizona or Texas. His gang caught hell and sustained many deaths in his absence. Many on his team accused him of being a coward and abandoning the gang, while others preferred, he go underground for protection. They valued his leadership and wanted him safe. Nonetheless, the Butcher Boys started to diminish and lose territory. They'd had no more loyalty and substance. They stood for nothing and therefore meant nothing. A house divided would always fall. There were a few stragglers and a few survivors, but for the most part, the Butcher Boys organization was finished.

As they faded, the 50/50 Crew flourished. Uzi Malik and Shotgun Shawn got promoted and, placed in charge of the areas in Hillside that bordered the Weequahic section, and were formally controlled by the Butcher Boys. They immediately relocated their families to quiet rural areas of Hillside and bought them houses, where they could be cozy, comfortable, and most importantly, safe.

While their families got settled in, Malik and Shawn ran around the town putting things in their proper perspectives letting all the locals know the new order of things and who were the go-to-guys. Nobody sold any weight in Hillside and the 50/50 Crew had everything on smash. Pills, dope, coke, ratchets; they owned all of the bars or bought out all of the clubs. They flooded the small town with the most exotic strands of weed and kept the customers addicted to the generous amounts they dished out. Unquestionably, they were the ultimate resource and never ran out of anything.

One by one, the competition either migrated or faded away. The 50/50 Crew didn't accept defectors in their organization because they didn't trust or have faith in anyone outside of the family. Whenever a member of the Butcher Boys was caught anywhere, he was made an example of and killed in the worst way. No one knew or could come up with any information as to the whereabouts of Baby Hatchet. He was long gone and showed no signs of returning to Essex County.

As Hillside fell under 50/50 Crew rule, so did some parts of Irvington. As is it was, more bodies were dropping left and right, and two more 50/50 Crew casualties, as Young Lateef and light-skinned Terry were ambushed at a drop-off/pick-up point, and both shot in the back of the head after being tied up to chairs. For everyone casualty on the 50/50 Crew's end, the Butcher Boy stragglers suffered at least five. The streets were filled with chaos, bullet holes, and bloodshed. It was one of the worst drug wars in recent memory. Over sixty bodies, three bombings, five rapes, four kidnappings, and countless aggravated assaults were committed within eighteen months.

Police were trying to protect and serve but were always one step behind. There was raid after raid, and search after search when word spread that the commissioner on down, were firing anyone not productive in the mission to bring down these murdering drug dealers. Arrest after arrest came day after day, and the bullpens were flooded with convicts and criminals. Tension would often build up when too many dudes from the same area ended up in the same space at the same time. They would begin to terrorize the weak and respect the stronger fellas up in the joint.

There was much money to be got in jail just like the streets, and even more so because the demand was much greater due to the scarceness of products. Whoever had the pipeline controlled shit everywhere despite the gangs and cliques throughout, and even incarcerated they were the bosses. If a motherfucker got hit up, seventy percent of the time it had something to do with one of the bosses. The rest of the incidents were just the general population doing the regular.

The 50/50 Crew had a large stake in the prison system as well. They would flood the correctional facilities and the major prisons in Jersey with heroin and weed. Just as they didn't play any games in the free world, they didn't play any games or take any shorts in the system. Motherfuckas got touched, straight up, if not murdered then stabbed or burnt the fuck up and shipped to another jail by way of the hospital. The ongoing war continued in the correctional systems from the streets of Newark and Irvington, and many were wounded during these jail wars, because most of the time they didn't expect the extreme drama and were caught off guard. Bodies were left in the corridors and found in the nooks of the stairwells of some joints, murdered by jailhouse shivs or strangled to death. Some officers and even some brass were on the extensive payroll of the 50/50 Crew and other major organizations behind the wall and resulting in many prison crimes being unsolved just as Speechless wanted it.

Twelve
Dangerous Business

Before Salvatore Calzonetti was murdered, he had given his apprentice three assignments. Three contracts that were worth three hundred grand each. Speechless was financially well-off and didn't need the payouts, but he was richer in loyalty and therefore felt obligated to fulfill those contracts that had been paid in advance, as Sal had always done. At first, it was a power move to keep Speechless indebted to him, but over time he simply came to trust that Speechless always got the job done.

If that weren't enough of a reason, Speechless felt connected to his mentor whenever he was out on a mission taking care of business. He could hear Sal's Italian-American accent calmly calling him son whether he was correcting or praising him. Sal was a large reason why Speechless was shaped into a force to be reckoned with and grew into a remorseless terror to those he would encounter and eliminate. Sal's handprint was woven through his existence, and it was hard to move past the realization that that chapter of life was forced closed, but he vowed to make it count.

The next target to be murdered were two brothers named Alfonso and Demetrius Maradino, competitors of the Canelli Crime family for years. They were allies that became enemies and had cost the Canelli family millions because of their connections with the Chinese and the pure heroin that they supplied.

Demetrius and his older brother Alfonso were five years apart in age, and worlds apart when it came to style. The only thing they had in common was their lust for more wealth and success. Originally from Greece, they adopted the name Maradino after they annihilated an entire clan of Maradinos during a three-year-long war for power. They made sure that no one survived or would ever continue the lineage of the Maradino Crime family, and had done so successfully.

After the last massacre at a private Maradino Family reunion, the brothers were satisfied that they had finished off their rivals. They migrated to the United States and immediately began to build their empire through restaurants, strip malls, and techno dance clubs that were havens and distribution centers for the constant demand for heroin, cocaine, and ecstasy pills.

Everywhere the two brothers went, they each were escorted by two professionally trained bodyguards that were licensed to carry firearms. They were both compulsive gamblers and loved betting on horses. They were popular in Atlantic City and Las Vegas, as well as all the known racetracks, and they'd won a lot of money as a result of always betting big.

Alfonso, the more casual of the brothers, always wore silk, satin, or suede tracksuits accompanied by designer tennis shoes by Fendi, Gucci, and other brand designers. If they made it, he bought it and wore it well. He even wore all-black Gucci sneakers and Gucci sweatsuits to funerals whenever he attended them.

His younger brother, on the other hand, was often mistaken as the older one because he wore a beard and always dressed in expensive tailor-made suits. Annually, he spent hundreds of thousands of dollars on shoes, suits, and imported ties. He was dapper and always dressed to impress no matter when, where or why.

Still, bachelors at ages thirty and thirty-five neither had children because they believed wives and children hindered a businessman of their magnitude and survival in their line of work. Familial ties were a liability more than a blessing and one luxury neither brother cared for.

During an art exhibit in New York City, the Maradino Brothers were escorted by two models from Miami and of course and security detail. As they had always done, they bragged about their acquired wealth and greater aspirations of corporate takeovers. They talked about the cars, homes, and horses they owned, in attempts to impress the lovely ladies and anyone within earshot. The brothers exaggerating their fame and fortune to clueless models had been their norm and for forty-eight thousand dollars, the paid escorts had better lavish the brothers with expressions and sentiments of being highly impressed and attracted, along with some head.

When the gala was over, one of the bodyguards had sent for their cars as they whispered into the ears and necks of the unsuspecting vixens. None of them, not even the highly paid security detail, suspected that the elder sheik with the turban and long beard, rolling along in an electronic wheelchair was Speechless in disguise. He had turned his gigantic size into an old, paralyzed cripple and hid in plain sight in almost every room the Maradino brothers visited during the tour.

When the valet drivers pulled up, there were two identical Maybach 62 luxury sedans, white on white with jet-black tinted windows and white shades drawn across the back and rear window. As they got into the luxurious homes on wheels and pulled off, Speechless rolled himself in the opposite direction and pulled out a detonator disguised as a cell phone. Highly explosive bombs had been discretely secured onto the mufflers of the Maybachs. They were three traffic lights from the Civic Center as the drivers pulled up side by side to the corner.

As Demetrius opened the private refrigerator, it triggered a sensor that sent a signal to the device Speechless held. He hit the call button and immediately, the two luxury automobiles exploded in the middle of traffic, destroying the cars directly in front and to the rear of the targeted vehicles, obliterating anything or anyone in the near vicinity. The bombs killed twenty-three people including the Maradino Brothers, their drivers and bodyguards, the two models, pedestrians crossing on the crosswalk, passengers in nearby vehicles, and a few others in the wrong place at the wrong time.

After disposing of his camouflage, Speechless calmly climbed into a car he had rented for the day using an alias and drove off into the night. After relaxing with Patricia for a few days, he was back in business mode. Seek and destroy was the mission. No remorse and no hesitation as he prepared for his next assignment.

His second target in the last package he received from Salvatore was a well-known figure in the mob and someone Speechless was already acquainted with. Frank Imperioletti, mob underboss to Don Vito Canelli and one of the ones responsible for Sal's death.

Why he was on the list was a mystery that Salvatore took to the grave, but nevertheless, Speechless had been paid for exterminating him, and a job was a job. He didn't believe in coincidences and knew it was destined for him to assassinate Frank for the murder and mutilation of his second father and mentor Salvatore Calzonetti and now because it was business, and worth three hundred thousand dollars.

He began tailing Frankie for three weeks straight during which, he'd familiarized Frank's routine, day in and day out. When he picked up money, when he dropped it off, when he ate, and when he used the bathroom. He became a shadow, unseen but able to see everything.

On an average morning on an average day, Frank Imperioletti walked to his doorstep to get the morning paper. As he gripped the doorknob, he heard a loud ticking sound. He searched for the source of the ticking and saw a bomb counting down with only twenty seconds before detonation. Frank frantically rattled the doorknob in an attempt to free himself, but his hand was glued to it.

As he heard the loud countdown start from twenty and begin to descend, he panicked even more, using his feet to try and pry himself from the door. He closed his eyes and said a last-minute prayer just as his bodyguards came running with their knives and pistols drawn after hearing their boss's screams. His prayers were the last words he ever spoke. The timer hit zero and the entire front of the estate, along with part of the roof was completely blown to pieces along with Frank Imperioletti.

THIRTEEN
THE GATHERING OF FAMILY

S peechless decided that everyone should take some time off and relax after the recent events. They all agreed and decided to vacation together in Miami, Florida for a month soaking up the sun and enjoying all the diversions Miami had to offer including the nightlife and restaurants. They rented three beach houses and drove their bullet-proof vehicles because they were always on guard. Even on vacation. Speechless and Patricia, along with Gorilla and his wife stayed at one beach house. Nearby, Pretty Boy, his family, and Short Slice shared a beach house, while Chinky, Uzi Malik, and Shotgun Shawn and their girls shared the third. They were looking forward to enjoying family and friends, no drama. No big machine guns, or bullet-proof suits. No beef, just peace,

But Speechless was never far away from business in his thoughts and plans. Every few days or so he would hold meetings in clubs or renting hotel suites just to have sit-downs and discuss the business back home and what was on their minds. Well respected was what they were, anywhere they went on the globe, and they always extended mutual respect to those selective few.

On one particular night, everybody from the 50/50 Crew rolled up in the building, coming through mobbed-up deep in a hot, well-known club, entering VIP as if they owned it. Close by a drunk yelled, 'Fucking Nigger!' before he and his entourage laughed out loud. Gorilla was close enough to the person to know where it came from, so he instinctively grabbed the millionaire heir by the throat and mushed the shit out of him! Everybody stopped in their tracks and swarmed in on what was going on.

Before they knew it a brawl ensued involving the white millionaire, his friends, bodyguards, club bouncers, and patrons. Everybody got the signal to bail and started to jet towards anything looking like an exit. The 50/50 crew were fighting dudes off as they grabbed onto them, trying to pull them to the ground to get stomped and trampled on.

Once outside and briefly accounted for, they realized that Uzi Malik wasn't there with the rest of them. Immediately Speechless and Gorilla ran back into the fight snuffing everything moving in the face and collarbone, rendering them dazed and hurt as they looked for their comrade. They saw Malik with his knife out getting jumped by four white boys. They had him surrounded so that he couldn't flee.

Quickly, Speechless and Gorilla pulled out icepicks and started poking anybody close to Uzi Malik, stabbing motherfuckas anywhere and everywhere. Once they saw that Malik hadn't taken any injuries that would prevent him from walking, they were out fast. Everybody took off and regrouped around the corner from the scene and agreed on meeting down at the beach houses.

Things were a lot safer and serene down by the water and sand, and Speechless wished he had spent more time down here and not only on vacations. He and Patricia went for a walk along the beach, hand in hand playfully bumping bodies as they slowly paced the length of the sand.

She talked about her ambitions, and he listened. She wanted to achieve success in the field she was in and her desire to be greater and above-average fueled her passion and increased her drive to achieve. She wanted to become a Federal agent. She wanted to work directly for the government, and she wanted to be the best at her profession. She knew how hard it was to be a woman and succeed at the professional level, so she was prepared to go that extra length to attain her goals. She talked about the academy and rumors about the training she had acquired through conversations here and there; rumors about the seriousness of it all, and the tests one was put through to prove themselves. It was as if her heart danced every time, she mentioned the bureau and the next level of law enforcement.

Speechless listened to her, loving that she was so ambitious. It was sexy for a woman to have as much drive as he had. But he couldn't help but wonder how it would all play out. Her succeeding in her ambitions would be a major risk or reward for his own. There was no use in worrying about it now. For now, he just wanted to be lost in the moment with her and present life.

CHINKY

Meanwhile, Chinky and Shotgun Shawn waited for Uzi Malik to come downstairs so that could go shoot some pool, play some cards, drink, and talk some shit with Shorty Slice. They always enjoyed kicking back and hanging out. There was no hatred amongst them and no animosity. Everybody got money and lived well, so there was no need for the bullshit that came with being in a crew. Most crews had different cliques within different families. Little spin-off sects that gravitated towards one another more than the general grew itself. That's how jealousy morphed to murder and murder led to promotion and eventually civil war. The 50/50 Crew had none of that negativity within their organization therefore, they didn't have those problems. Everybody was treated like family.

Shawn and Shorty started with shots of tequila and a fifty-dollar-ball game of pool. The cost was fifty dollars plus every ball that remained once your opponent sank the eight ball would cost the loser and an additional fifty dollars each. Chinky and Malik were at the other table shooting nine-ball for a hundred dollars a ball. Malik was beating the hell out of Chinky and was up about eighteen stacks within the first three games. Shawn and Shorty Slice were going back and forth game for game, but Shawn maintained the financial edge over his little bro who always left at least four balls on the table whenever he lost.

Once they played a few rounds they talked their way to the poker table to play some Texas Hold 'Em with a two-thousand-dollar minimum buy-in, unlimited max., and twenty-five to fifty-dollar blinds. Everybody started ten grand eager to take the next homeboy's stack right off the back. Chinky was a very aggressive player and always made people fold by betting heavily from the very first card. Either he lost a lot of money in a hand, or he won a lot of money in a hand. He didn't care about the comments and mumbles, or how people felt when he bet the way he did. Go big or go home was how he played.

Anybody that ever won a hand against him was very happy, they had no complaints. You had to take the good with the bad and not regret anything when you are gambling, especially if you're in it for the hustle, and not just the mere sport of playing cards. The usual outcome, Chinky went up about twenty-grand on them and then quit while he was ahead. Malik and Shawn were pissed off because they were down the most money when he quit. They'd never played with him before, so they didn't expect it or see that move coming. He cashed out and shot some pool by himself waiting for this Cuban doll to come through and pick him up, in her Maserati convertible she bragged about so much.

She boasted about how the rim color and paint job matched in all white during the day but at night would glow like a lavender spaceship. Chinky was amused at how she could explain things with such enthusiasm and newfound excitement as if he had never heard or seen the shit she described. She was cute. He had done this same shit with at least four of his cars two years before meeting her, but she was funny, so he'd let her think she was impressing him.

When she finally did pull up to get him, it did appear as though she was cruising in a spacecraft, because of the backdrop of the ocean at night, and the fact that you really couldn't see the ground. When she stopped the car, she got out so that he could inspect her efforts and appreciate her completeness. She also asked him did he want to drive, which he declined like a seasoned Mack and told her that he would rather be shown the city. They cruised on Ocean Drive and took in the sights, and of course Chinky acted astonished, like he had never been outside of Newark, New Jersey before, although his passport had numerous stamps on it. She showed him numerous areas of Dade County, including Carol City and the Pork & Bean Projects.

All Chinky did was check out potential territory and links to the city of Miami because he always had money on his mind and his mind was always on money. He was sizing up Ms. Cuba, Cindy Cruz, and seeing how far she would possibly go to be on his team because that's what he did with any and every bad bitch he ever fucked with. There was no hidden agenda. Resources were always his objectives. Top-notch diamond broads always had the scoop on what was jumping in the town or who was popular, who was making and getting what? He would milk this bitch for all the info worthy of listening to, and before they flew home in a few weeks, he would have a dangerously beautiful lady on his team in Miami.

At the Hilton, Cynthia Cruz and Chinky got real familiar. They fucked and talked, ate, fucked and talked some more, then fucked again after breakfast. He called his partners to check in and let them know everything was everything, and that hadn't been set up as they had teased, he would be.

In the morning, Cindy and Chinky walked on the beach and talked about many things. He had a player side to him without a doubt, and had been talking women out of their panties since he was a young teenager. Being black and Vietnamese had its advantages, and his street swagger was what put the package altogether. No matter how long women were around him or how many fell in love with him, Chinky would never love them back. He only loved what they could do for him. The better they listened and followed protocol by sticking to the script, the longer he kept them around. He was all about that money, money, and more money.

After strolling on the beach, Cindy took him shopping for Gucci swimwear and loungewear and then spent a little change on him at the Polo store. He had to admit, he was not used to females taking him shopping and spending a few bands on him. The most he'd gotten was some nice footwear with an official outfit, and maybe a cap for less than a stack. Cindy was really putting in overtime and treating him the way he deserved to be respected and admired. He could see her being his chick away from home and her getting her hands dirty. She had ride or die potential.

SPEECHLESS

After the nightclub disaster, the 50/50 Crew would occasionally meet up somewhere on the beach at a secluded spot they chose for themselves and would discuss business, current, and future. Speechless expressed to everyone that there was tremendous potential for the crew in Miami and that they could invest in a few businesses in Miami: nightclubs, barbershops, and restaurants. Everyone was excited and looking forward to the future direction of the 50/50 Crew, shit they loved Florida.

"I'm telling you family, this town, this state can be the next plateau for us. We can own this fucking town and expand our empire greatly." When it came to expansion Speechless had more than enough to say.

"That sounds like a great idea," Gorilla tugged at his beard, a sign he was listening attentively. "We can retire down this bitch, and we don't have to get chubby either," he joked with a big grin on his face.

"You all are family to me. The only family I have, and it will always be that way homeboys." Pretty Boy nodded, his facial smooth expression calm as always. "Whatever is good for the team, I'm down. I'm in all the way. Til death and then some my brothers. Every person in this cipher right here, I would die for. Twice. Believe that."

"We already know Pretty Boy," Shorty Slice interjected. "Nigga you have been there for me more times than my own family has been, so I don't doubt your devotion for a second, Playboy. Shit, we have all been to hell and came back with million-dollar raincoats on!"

"Let's do this! Whenever you all are ready, just say the word and heads will roll down this motherfucker. I got youngsters that erase entire families for a hundred stacks on deck. They ready whenever and wherever, to get whoever."

"We still got to tie up a lot of loose ends back home though. Still, I'm ready when you are Speechless. Just say the word big dog." Chinky sat forward his elbows on his knees like an eager student on the first day of class except Chinky was well-schooled in building street empires.

"We need this and then some. Me and Malik are family for life with you brothers," said Shotgun Shawn, "and nothing is ever going to change that. You gave us new life when shit was so critical, Boss Man".

"Man, you two motherfuckas earned them stripes and put work in like everybody standing in front of you. Cut that shit out Shawn," Speechless wasn't the sentimental type but he certainly gave props when they were due.

"Yeah, but at a time when nobody was listening or gave a shit about our potential, you were there Speechless. It was you that gave us a chance to prove ourselves. And for that we owe you forever big bro," said Uzi Malik from Bergen Street. Shawn nodded in agreement and dabbed his boy.

"We family now. Now light up that good-good, and let's smoke to the future," said the boss.

FOURTEEN

THE TAKEOVER

After Miami, the 50/50 Crew decided to put an end to any drama or unfinished business that they had with anyone. It was back to business as usual. Cash needed to be paid, debts were due, and lives were still owed from Frank Imperioletti's accomplices in the murder of his side-wifey, Tammy. The captains made their selected rounds in their designated territories and collected what was due.

There was suddenly conflict when Pretty Boy went to collect fifteen bands from this Dominican cat. Not only was he told that he wasn't getting his money, but he was jumped by four Dominicans and left battered by the side of a liquor store. When Speechless got the news, he called Pretty Boy to his house to have a one-on-one. They drank and smoked, then kicked it.

"Pretty Boy, you my little brother, and I love you to death so anything you want done to those clowns is considered done yesterday." Speechless was not letting anyone get away with beating down a captain. Not only because he honored his 50/50 Crew but also because lack of retaliation showed weakness. If one person got away with disrespect, soon others would follow. There was no way Speechless could allow the 50/50 Crew to look weak. "These motherfuckas violated family and they are going to pay. No question. But it's your decision how because it's your territory that is going to suffer financially for a while from the heat. Just tell me what's up?"

"Speechless, bro you know that I'm all about the family and this money and I love my brothers like we came from the same pussy, but fuck that territory. I want all these motherfuckers dead big brother. Straight like that! I ain't playin' no motherfuckin' games. They want this headache, now they got more than they can handle. Fuck that shit!" Pretty Boy was usually so calm he could've been a corpse. Even when he wasn't high as fuck on bud, his natural demeanor was chill mode. To hear him yelling meant he was angry beyond limits.

"They die in the morning." Speechless, with anger seething through his eyes said calmly before he passed Pretty Boy a blunt to help calm him.

Pretty Boy accepted it but didn't bring it to his lips. He stared into his big brother's eyes. "I gotta be there when it happens."

Speechless nodded once. That was only right.

Early the next morning, four young Dominican gangsters were eating breakfast at a neighborhood diner before they went to hustle on the block at seven o'clock when six masked men ran inside and opened fire on them. The hoods that the shooters wore made them look like a group of grim reapers, and the fire coming from the nozzles of the AR 15's made it look like a bloody movie scene. Hundreds of bullets smashed and shattered bodies, tables, chairs, and widows in the booth they were in and the two on each side.

Each shooter reloaded his weapon, and then pumped the remains of that second clip into the bodies as well. The assassins ran toward the exit, almost stumbling and tripping over one another, until a shot rang out, and one of the shooters went down from a fatal wound to the back of the head. After that everyone quickly stopped, turned, and opened fire with 9mm automatic handguns toward the source of the gunfire.

Primo, the motherfucker that owed Pretty Boy the loot in the first place had been hiding in the bathroom the entire time. When Pretty Boy spotted him, he loaded a hundred-shot clip into the AR 15, jumped over the body of his dead comrade, and shot Primo emptying the clip. The barrage of gunfire knocked him back several feet and tore his body apart completely, he was nothing but a bloody pulp of what use to be a human being when Pretty Boy was finished with him. As they jumped the steps the silence seemed foreign to them. Shotgun Shawn was usually going off at the mouth by now saying something. Anything. It was his way of coping with the terroristic lifestyle of a cold-blooded killer. He would ease the edge by hearing his own voice, during or after jobs. Everyone stopped at the getaway trucks and paused taking account of who was there then Uzi Malik let out an angry yell and punched the car.

"My fucking bro! That motherfucker killed Shawn!" He paced and screamed out his anger before he faced his comrades. "That piece of shit's family dies for this shit, my niggas. Believe that!"

As the day moved on the reports reached the entire 50/50 Crew family, that they had lost a dear brother in the field, and at only twenty-five years old. Everybody was grief-stricken and sick behind the blind-sided killing of their homie. They vowed to retaliate severely. The next day before services would start the following week for Shotgun Shawn, Primo and his family members' houses were all blown up. His mother, sister, uncle, and the mother to his children were all targeted. A total of thirty bodies including twelve children were among the casualties.

Shawn Shotgun Miller was laid to rest at Perry's Funeral Home on High Street in Newark, New Jersey at 10:04 in the morning on a Saturday. Anybody that knew him or knew of him came out to pay their respects. He was survived by his wife Sharon and their five-year-old son Shawn Jr. also known as Little Shottie. Everyone from the 50/50 Crew pitched in and gave his wife and child a million-dollar cash care package, made sure that they were set up real nice in Atlanta, and assigned two younger shooters to live down there to always watch over Sharon and her son. Speechless was like that when it came to family.

Shotgun Shawn was entombed near Hillside, New Jersey in a mausoleum paid for, reserved, and dedicated to the high-ranking members of the 50/50 Crew. It was a decision they collectively made when Shawn was killed that they would be together, even in death.

After the services, after everyone had milled out and went about their business, it was time to celebrate Shotgun Shawn's life with those closest to him. There were cases of expensive champagne, boxes of cognac and vodka, ounces and ounces of different exotic weed to smoke, along with four boxes of Dutch Masters.

Uzi Malik had taken Shawn's death harder than anyone in the 50/50 Crew because they were childhood friends from the Weequahic section and had been partners in crime for well over ten years. It was Shawn who first taught Malik how to shoot a pistol properly and how to rob a motherfucka with just fear, and no gun being drawn at all. Sometimes in Newark, New Jersey a reputation could get you far, and sometimes it could get you killed. If you were around a bunch of doe-getters that feared you and they were always worried that you might stick them up, nine times out of ten you could end up dead if you were not strapped or armed with something.

They'd gotten so skilled that Shawn and Malik were well respected and equally feared in the hood known for their skills in robbery, murder-for-hire, and kidnapping. Shawn had even given Malik the nickname Uzi, because of Malik's infatuation with the semiautomatic compact machine gun where his name was an homage bestowed upon him from an O.G. that once saw him blow an older gangster's leg off with a shotgun for disrespecting his mother. Afterward, he'd run to Malik's to stash the gun. It was one of the many stories they shared.

For weeks, every day seemed empty without Shotgun Shawn. Uzi Malik would tend to go on "solo missions to keep his mind occupied and to cope with the grief." He would strap up heavy, and just go into the territory of known enemies with murderous intentions. In two weeks, he had accumulated eight bodies. In his rampage he was just laying motherfuckas down left and right and killing whomever he caught slipping with their guard down. He did it for his brother Shawn. He did it for closure.

In the process of grieving through retaliation, Malik crossed too many people associated with men in high places. As a result, a hundred grand contract had been put out on him by the Nigerians who ran heroin through Newark and who also wanted his body dead or alive. One of his victims had been a top earner for the Nigerians and his death created a void in the market and an eventually mini-war for the now available turf. The Africans took messing with their bottom dollar as a slap in the face and wanted nothing more than to be responsible for Uzi Malik's demise.

Within a week, there had been two attempts on Malik's life. The first was when he was leaving the mall and was almost run over by a heavy-duty pick-up truck. The second attempt took place at the movie theater on Route 22. His car had been riddled with bullets after Malik had set up a decoy. He had positioned his hoodie by hanging the hood on the headrest from the rear giving the interior the appearance that someone was actually in the vehicle.

Speechless didn't waste any time when the last attempt was made on Malik's life. He decided to get him out of town as soon as possible. The Nigerians would be dealt with severely. Despite their power and apparent unlimited wealth, they violated a member of the 50/50 Crew. The penalty was death.

"Malik, you have got to get low for a while so I'm sending you to Miami to relax for a year until this thing is settled, and your mental is clear of Shotgun Shawn's death." Speechless was telling not asking. "I know that you miss the shit out of Florida anyway. We all do Malik, and besides, we can get an early jumpstart on the plans we have for the expansion. Take this suitcase, it has two mini 45 automatics that come with four clips and two boxes of hollow-tipped bullets. There is nearly six hundred grand from your brothers and me to help get you situated down there. The pound of loud smoke is from Pretty Boy because he knows how you like to choke when you are not working or doing a job!" Speechless teased with a broad grin on his face.

"Don't worry about your personal bank account. You don't have to touch that money. It will be there when your vacation is over."

"I appreciate everything Speechless, and I didn't mean to bring drama to the family that could have been avoided. I just fucking snapped, and I miss my partner, my brother, my friend 'til the motherfucking end. I swear to you that I will be good when I finally get back to Newark and that I am going to make the best out of this time in Florida. Whatever you need me to do down there, consider it done. My love and loyalty runs deep for this family and no matter what, my brothers come first. My wife and kids are going to enjoy this extended vacation, and the children are dying to visit Disney World again anyway." Malik grinned before he sobered. "Thanks for everything, Bro."

"It's nothing, Malik. You are family and we take care of ours. Point. Blank. Period. You don't have to thank me or thank your brothers. Shit like this comes automatically when one of us needs to disappear for a while. Court cases, bodies, witness disposal, relentlessly vindictive girlfriends or wives, etc. Whatever the scenario, we get our people out of town immediately, then whatever or whoever has to be dealt with can be focused on. I thank you for offering the apology because I know that your intentions are genuine, but you owe us no explanation. You hear me?!"

Then they shook hands, embraced one another in the traditional 50/50 Crew two-arm hug before they lit up a blunt of the best sour diesel in the entire Essex County, and talked about the future.

FIFTEEN
KARMA

UZI MALIK

One of the private jets that the 50/50 Crew used for family getaways and emergency exits landed at Miami Airport safely as usual, and Uzi Malik emerged from the G5 Gulfstream with a Gucci carryon. His wife walked off with a Louis Vuitton tote clutched in one hand and her daughter's hand in the other while their son followed behind. They checked into a plush hotel on the strip of Ocean Drive. Afterward, Malik called a locksmith to have special reinforced locks added to the hotel suite as an extra security measure. He gave the hotel manager an additional ten grand for the leniency and his understanding of Malik's concern for his family.

After two weeks in Florida, Malik stepped out on the scene and began to scope the prime real estate for business. He was cruising around in a rented Mercedes S550 when he could have sworn, he saw the bad bitch that Chinky was fucking with months ago. She was riding in a fucking Gallardo convertible with bitch ass Baby Hatchet from the Butcher Boys clique. He got on the jack immediately and called Speechless as he U-Turned to follow the white Lambo.

"Speechless, I'm telling you, Bro, bitch-ass motherfucka Baby Hatchet is down here rolling some kind of heavy, and he is with the exotic broad that Chinky wrapped up when we were all down here on my first major family vacation. The bitch is giving this pussy head in broad daylight with the top down. He must have this hoe on lock down, so we have to get to that bitch as soon as possible."

"Malik, don't lose him. Stay with him and be careful. Wet his ass up if he tries to get the drop on you and don't fucking hesitate because if he has an organization established down there, then we need to chalkboard all of them bitches." Speechless's voice was calm and steady, but his words packed dynamite. "Stay in touch with all things regarding him. I want the whole schedule and rundown on him and his movement. I'm going to send you some assistance ASAP. They'll are on the next thing flight to Miami. They'll contact you when they land."

"Ok, Big Bro. I will stick to him like Velcro and still be discreet. You already know how I do." Malik followed Baby Hatchet and his bitch to a spot that looked like what could be a stash house, then he watched from a safe distance as they both needed to carry the huge sack into the building. The contents were either drugs, money, or both. After a half-hour, Baby Hatchett and the broad emerged from the abandoned warehouse building and headed toward a gated community lined with townhouses.

Once Malik observed them parking and getting out of the convertible, he jetted back to his room to grab his high-powered binoculars and told his wife to start looking for a townhouse to rent in Orlando ASAP. His wife and kids had to leave Miami immediately. Then he headed back out towards the townhouses that harbored one of the 50/50 Crew's most wanted enemies.

With his long-range binoculars, Uzi Malik intently honed in on the general area where the white dropped top Gallardo was parked, waiting for nearly two hours for either one of them to appear and reveal their location. He called Speechless and put the phone on speaker so that he wasn't to be distracted while looking through the binoculars.

"What's it looking like little brother?" Speechless's tone sounded bored as always, but Malik knew better than that. That tone meant Speechless was focused. Plotting and thinking. He had too much going on in life to ever be bored. Or he was around someone who didn't need to know any details about this new development. "Any new developments in that important matter we discussed?"

"Indeed bro. I observed some serious moves being made between these two and now I am posted outside of what seems to be their honeycomb hideout at some posh gated community." Malik paused when he saw a garage door open. When he saw a middle-aged man in golfing clothes step out and walk to his mailbox, Malik relaxed and got back to business not spotting Hatchet or the girl. "What's up with my scouts?"

"They are in route. We had to fly them down in the GS4 muddy waters. Their ETA is a few minutes from now. They've been in the air for a while. They know you are in charge so don't hesitate to give them orders. They are coming up as you and Shawn, may he rest in peace, did. And they are just as loyal."

Malik took in everything Speechless divulged with little words as he always did. Malik doubted anyone could rise in ranks and loyalty as he and Shawn had but he took the information for what it was worth. Two soldiers coming in strapped and could be trusted was all he needed to hear.

Gritty and Grimy touched down in Miami with no problems and called Malik immediately so that he could pick them up, but he told them to wait for the limo to pick them up and take them to their hotel. Once they reached the hotel suite, the two twenty-year-old identical twin brothers unloaded their luggage and their arsenal and ordered room service. The twins ate all of what they had ordered, and then smoked on some extremely loud purple before meeting up with Uzi Malik.

Malik called the twins and told them when and where to meet him. As instructed, they each pulled up in separate Ubers, ordered from two different make-believe rooms, and arrived three minutes apart. When they were finally together Malik could see the remarkable resemblance as they approached him, although one had spinning waves in his hair and the other, Gritty, was bald.

They looked exactly the same, even down to the identical scar under their left eyes given to each from the same dude they both fought twice when they were all fourteen years old. Until they got together finally and killed him. Their first of many murders. They were wild as shit, and ever since they were twelve, they were little terrors in the neighborhood and didn't take any shit from anyone.

Always in trouble for fighting, little Gritty the older of the two constantly got suspended and eventually expelled from school. They plotted and planned and lured the bigger bully into an alley, when they were just fourteen, and beat him to death with baseball bats. Afterward, they covered his body with garbage and waste from the alley and fled the scene, never to be found out or even investigated for the crime.

When they walked up to Uzi Malik they spoke in unison. "What's good Uzi?"

"What's the plan big bro, and where do you need us?"

"Everything will be good once this motherfucker is in the fucking dirt. Do you hear what I'm saying? We have orders and directions from the family. So, we do whatever we have to do to get this shit done." Malik watched them closely.

Gritty nodded confidently. "Alright." He extended his hand. "I'm Gritty and this is my brother Grimy. We from Hooterville. Up the hill, Pine Grove Terrace, and South Orange Avenue. Born and raised. We have been family with the 50/50 Crew for about a year now and everyone knows how we get down. We don't fucking play. The boss man said come help out and assist big brother Malik down the bottom, so here we are my people. Just tell us what to do and point us in the right direction. Whatever you need done, we go above and beyond the call of duty. We motherfuckin' soldiers." Gritty and Grimy dabbed each other nodding in agreement.

Grimy lifted his chin. "That's all we know is puttin' in work. Since back in the day. We will be keeping shit regulated for you and the family while we are here, for as long as you need us to be. We don't have kids or wives, and we don't get attached to shit except our family in these streets!"

"Ok, ok. I feel your energy little gangster and I respect what you're saying to the fullest degree. You and your brother have to move when I say move and shoot when I say fire you hear me?" Uzi Malik could feel the violence radiating off them in waves. Dangerous if they lost control. He spoke sternly, asserting his leadership while staring at the twins stone-faced. The twins nodded their heads in unison as Malik closed out his concise oration and crash course of rules.

As the three of them sat in the air-conditioned confines of the car, Uzi Malik, and the twins watched the apartment that Baby Hatchet and Ms. Cuba occupied. They patiently waited for the couple to surface. When they appeared a few hours later, they were both decked out. As they walked towards the Lamborghini Gallardo convertible, the twins were antsy as hell and eager to jack them, rob, and murder them as soon as Malik gave the word.

"Relax young bloods. The orders are to follow, observe, and report. We only kill these motherfuckers if threatened at this point, until Speechless says different. Understand?"

"Man, we can rush them motherfuckers right now. Take them back in the spot, and get everything we need and finish this shit!" Exclaimed Grimy.

"Word up Malik," Gritty agreed.

"You two trigger happy motherfuckers better be easy and just keep your eyes on all things as we tail these two lamb chops. And don't worry. We are going to eat real soon, little brothers," Uzi Malik promised as he pulled out onto the road and trailed at a safe distance.

Cynthia "Ms. Cuba" Cruz drove the smooth vehicle as Baby Hatchet talked on the phone with his ankles crossed and hanging out the window. It was hot as hell outside, and everywhere they drove they could see motorcycles and convertibles with their tops down.

For the twins, it was also a sight-seeing trip as well as a vacation, because they had never been out of Newark, except to commit robbery/murders in Jersey City or New York City. They never really gave a fuck about traveling anywhere. They were just hood born, hood raised, and hood bound. They both sported tattoos that read Property of Brick City. Gritty was tatted on the right side of his neck and Grimy on his breastplate, directly below his collarbone. They would probably kill somebody just for saying something disrespectful about their hometown.

Uzi tailed them to another spot, where they came back out with two more stuffed duffel bags then drove to what he assumed was the drop-off location once they came out with just a small briefcase. Afterward, they took off in the Gallardo and started accelerating a little faster than usual, dipping through traffic and picking up speed. Baby Hatchet was behind the wheel since the last drop-off, possibly sensing something was up. Malik stayed with them but still at a distance. He was a veteran and could tell that Baby Hatchet had realized he picked up a tail. An S550 was not your average surveillance car and wasn't inconspicuous. They sped through traffic until they were caught at a red light, allowing Uzi Malik and the twins to ease closer.

Suddenly, Baby Hatchet turned around and started blasting away in the direction of Uzi Malik and the Twins. Ms. Cuba started doing the same, shattering the windshield and taking out the passenger side mirror with an onslaught of bullets. Immediately the Twins were ready, leaning out of the windows and shooting back whenever they could while avoiding being shot in return. Baby Hatchet and Cynthia sped off, but the Twins both said they hit their marks even if only superficial wounds.

They sped through the traffic signal with Uzi Malik and Twins in hot pursuit of them, bullets whizzing by their heads and some even hitting the upper frame of the car and shattering the rear-view mirror. The Twins, who were both armed with seventeen-shot Beretta 9mm handguns, kept up the relentless assault on them. They had shot out the passenger side mirror, as well as the rear-view mirror and back lights, and they were just beginning to reload.

Baby Hatchet took evasive action. Suddenly, the Gallardo swerved in and out of traffic at a speed clocking sixty-five miles per hour and gaining speed as it caught any length of the straightaway, where the Mercedes Benz could not go. Still, the twins keep the onslaught going and bullets were flying and hitting the exotic sports car as it careened in and out of traffic. A police cruiser sitting at a red light at the opposite end of the street waiting for the light to turn green was then alerted when a stray bullet scratched the hood of his squad car. He instantly turned on his lights and sirens and joined in on the chase.

"Oh shit! Malik! We got beast on us, and he is coming fast, Bro." Grimy yelled from the backseat reloading his weapon. "What you want me to do bruh? You want me to air this motherfucka out or what?"

"Do what the fuck you gotta do! Get that roller off our ass!" The bass in Uzi Malik's voice competed with the sirens and gunfire but Grimy heard his orders loud and clear. Eliminate!

"I got this!" he replied as he inserted a fresh full clip into the 9mm and started shooting at the cop car. Uzi hadn't seen what the twins were capable of up close but a quick look in the rearview and he knew Speechless sent the right soldiers. Grimy was a good shot. Twelve shots took out the windshield, disabled the radiator, and flattened the two front tires as the patrol car. It swerved out of control jumping the curb, destroying a mailbox, benches that were cemented to the sidewalk, and two Department of Motor Vehicles street signs before crashed into two storefronts and right into their front windows.

While Grimy was shooting at police, Baby Hatchet and Cynthia had accelerated their speed up to about eighty miles per hour and getting a good distance ahead of them. Two more cop cars came from one of the adjacent streets and began to chase the Lamborghini Gallardo, oblivious to Uzi Malik and the Twins in the Mercedes chasing and shooting at the fleeing convertible.

Immediately Uzi Malik turned off of the street they were on because he didn't want to pick up any extra heat that would recognize the car or the bullet holes in it and give chase.

"Fuck! Lucky motherfuckers!" Uzi Malik began banging on the steering wheel in frustration.

"Damn! We had them bitches man!" Gritty sat back frustrated.

"Yeah! We did! How the fuck? They lucky as shit that those cops saved their fucking ass because those motherfuckers were good as dead!" Grimy said, hyped up in the back.

"Let's ditch this motherfuckin' rental and report this bitch stolen ASAP. Then we get out of these motherfuckin' clothes." Uzi Malik didn't waste time dwelling on what was already done but instead kept moving forward with the ultimate goal. "We will see them again soon. We know where they are and some of their stash-houses too."

SIXTEEN
IT'S NOT OVER

After the murders of Frank Imperioletti and his bodyguards, the Don planned on going into seclusion, but not before issuing contracts and approving the green light for certain murders. The remote island he had purchased ten years ago, in the event he or his family was ever targeted to be whacked was located amongst the Fiji Islands. He would be comfortable and feel completely safe in his faraway private resort.

His compound was vast, boasting numerous streams and waterfalls, fresh fruit, and beautiful trees stretched far beyond eyesight. The view from the beautiful hilltops was breathtaking no matter which side of the island you were on. On this private little paradise, he had built a mini-mansion and five surrounding villas. Each villa was occupied by at least two heavily armed guards at all times during their stay. He also had live-in maids and Italian chefs, as well as ten South African Mastiffs that patrolled the grounds at all times. They lived on the island full-time training and breeding.

Of course, the Don trusted no one, so all of the maids, chefs, and groundskeepers, were all relatives of the Canelli family to some degree. The high-tech security system was manned by two of his trusted security experts who constantly watched for intruders on the seventeen-screen security monitor board that showed the entire fortress.

For decades, Don Vito Canelli ruled the New Jersey mafia in specific Northern cities within Essex County, as well as some major business ties in New York City and Florida. Still, he was no fool and did not become successful being stupid or ignorant. Both his son and his beloved grandson Joey Jr. were locked away for life, so he planned to get low and hide out, while the streets would run red with his enemies' gore.

He sent for his four capos and had a very concise private meeting. The meeting was a direct order to terminate anyone affiliated with the 50/50 Crew and their partnering crews on the streets of Newark, Irvington, Hillside, and East Orange. The meeting also disclosed that they would be expanding soon into Florida and Upstate New York, near the capitol. No questions were permitted at the meeting Don spoke his strict orders and that was all they needed to know.

SPEECHLESS

Speechless wanted more than anything, to kill Don Canelli and secure total dominance in the streets for his 50/50 Crew in the future. He knew that he was going to be linked to the streets forever because not only was he addicted to the money and the power, but it was a blood oath he and his partners had taken when they all became brothers. *'From the play yard to the graveyard, we get money and play hard!"*

That was the motto they lived by, and anyone blocking that dream was swiftly removed permanently. Every one of the founding five bosses Shorty Slice, Pretty Boy, Chinky, Gorilla, and Speechless had all placed their word on the code and would live by it for life.

Although they were extremely rich already, they were not wealthy, so their quest for financial retirement was far from complete. They had all agreed collectively that the businesses would prosper in other states besides New Jersey. With plans already in the works down in South Florida it would not take long for their expansion to prosper.

SEVENTEEN
REVELATION

Speechless talked with Uzi Malik regularly and was given a detailed update as to what was happening down there. His recent shootout with the 50/50 Crews' main nemesis Baby Hatchet, leader of the murderous Butcher Boys clique, had Speechless very upset.

"This motherfucker got away?" He asked infuriated. "You had the drop on him and his bitch, and you let them escape Malik? What's up with that? That's not like you bro?" Speechless went on chastising Uzi's lost opportunity.

"Nah, Big Bro we didn't let them do anything. The police saved their asses when we were closing in. We had them, and I am positive that they both caught a hot one somewhere on their bodies. The Twins are about their business for sure!"

"Are they listening to you down there? None of you got touched in that battle, right? You good?" asked Speechless relieved Uzi still was on top of his game and had a legitimate reason for failing.

"Yeah, I'm good. So are the young shooters. We didn't even get grazed, but we sent over sixty hot ones at them. Tore that Lambo they were riding in up. And we had to dump on a beast mobile to get the fuck on up out of there bro!" Uzi Malik recounted.

"Word?" asked Speechless. "You serious?" he asked again.

"No joke," replied Uzi Malik.

Speechless and his brothers were mad as a motherfucker, to know that a major enemy was still existing and trying to enterprise in an area that they had on their own radar, it was ordered that the matter be handled quickly and effectively, and the results indefinite.

They drove around Miami for hours every day, appearing to be a rap duo along with their manager or D.J., and they spent thousands to maintain their cover and remain incognito. Uzi Malik and the Twins spent days and nights looking for Baby Hatchet and his bitch everywhere they could think of, but it was as if they had just disappeared. The three of them decided to go to the mall for a little shopping excursion and chill out time, take a little break from the stakeouts, and all the driving around. They frequented the shopping scenes every day and strip clubs almost every night, but still, there was no sign of either of their targets. Against Uzi Malik's advice, the Twins decided to visit the food court and flirt with some down south bitches, who would be attracted to them because they always got extra attention whenever they were out and about. Twin attention.

As Uzi Malik went to grab a stack of Tru Jeans, the Twins yelled to him that they would be right back, and in an instant Malik's intuition jerked. Both brothers had serious addictions to Nathan's famous beef hotdogs and fries, and could not resist temptation when they saw the small franchise at the upper-level food court.

As the younger brother, Grimy ordered his food his brother was preoccupied with this lovely Latina with a skin-tight burgundy cat suit and matching burgundy cornrows flowing down her back. Her body resembled that of a famous video model from Canada, and she appeared as if someone had sketched her or something. Her tapered calves and thighs met with her voluptuous ass and perfect hips flawlessly, and her waist was tighter than an aerobics instructor.

"Yo, Bro! Look at shorty right there in the white heels and maroon body suit. Damn! She is tight my nigga and she is killing those pumps with the white Louie V headband on those braids. I like shorty style," said Gritty. "Hold me down Bro. I am going to scoop shorty real quick though. Watch me work my nigga."

114

As he went in the direction of the cutie, his brother turned back toward the menu to finish ordering their food.

"Excuse me *mami chula*. Can I get a minute of your time sweetheart?" Gritty asked in his up north accent while tapping her on the left shoulder. When she spun around, obviously bothered by the intrusion, he was completely shocked at the sight of her face and the recognition that registered. But it was too late. With expert quickness, in one fluid motion, she slipped a blade from under her tongue and swiped it across his throat before she turned in the opposite direction disappearing behind a group of shoppers.

Just as Grimy opened his mouth to order their food, a woman screamed behind him and froze him in mid-sentence.

When he turned toward the commotion, he saw his brother staggering towards him wide-eyed and fighting to keep closed the gaping wound that started at the left side of his neck. As Gritty struggled with all the strength he could muster to reach his brother, an uncontrollable amount of blood gushed everywhere. It squirted through the gaps of his fingers and oozed down his crisscrossed, tattooed forearms. They were inches from one another when the mortally injured Twin collapsed and began to convulse on the polished floor at his brother's feet.

"Twin!" screamed Grimy, overcome at the sight of his dying brother, as he quickly got down on the floor to help his brother. "Help! Somebody help us! Somebody help my brother! Please!" Over and over again he shouted for someone to do something instead of standing there watching his brother die.

Grimy's torso was covered in splattered blood as he held his older sibling staring into the fear in his widened eyes. It didn't take long before Gritty's body stopped convulsing and his lifeless hands fell to his chest. For what seemed like an eternity, Grimy just stared into his brother's now vacant eyes before he closed them ultimately willing his brother to rest in peace.

EIGHTEEN
PLAN UPGRADE

GRITTY AND GRIMY

Uzi Malik could not believe what had just happened in what seemed like a few minutes. One of the soldiers he was responsible for had just been murdered in broad daylight inside of one of the local malls, and now he had some serious questions to answer with the heads of the 50/50 Crew.

"Damn Twin! How the fuck does this shit happen son? How in the hell did this fucked up shit go down huh?" Asked Uzi Malik. He and the surviving twin sat outside in front of the coroners' office inside another rented Mercedes Benz and discussed what went wrong and who was responsible.

"It was a female Malik. Some bitch with burgundy cornrows and a mean ass body. You know my brother couldn't resist a bad bitch, Man." Grimy rubbed his head in disbelief. "I don't know what the fuck happened Big Bro. I had my eyes on him the whole time. Then as soon as I ordered our food, I heard some lady screaming loud as shit. Then I saw Gritty, and I could tell he was trying to tell me something."

"So, you didn't even see the bitches face? What does she look like? And why did you let your brother leave your side? You know better than that shit. We are not from out here, Dog. We never separate!" Barked Uzi Malik. "You two motherfuckers are supposed to be down here handling business instead of letting your guards down! Now, look at this fucking mess I have to answer for!"

"Nah Bro. I only saw the bitch from behind. I didn't even get a profile of her face man. This shit is crazy. I can't fucking believe my other half is gone, Man. That nigga completed me and now I won't feel whole again until whoever did this is fucking dead and gone! They killed the wrong motherfuckin' gangster, Malik. The wrong motherfuckin' gangster." Grimy's words trailed off as his lips began to quiver and tears formed in his eyes.

"One thing is for sure, and two things are for certain Twin, we are going to kill this motherfucker Baby Hatchet and this mystery bitch. I promise you that shit little bro!" Malik touched Twins' shoulder to assure him that justice would be done and offer condolences. He knew all too well what it felt like to lose somebody you were close to.

SPEECHLESS

Back home in Newark, word was getting back, and information was shared about the death of one of the twins. Everyone knew that his identical twin brother was taking this harder than anyone in the entire family, and they all knew he would be bent on retribution.

Speechless and Chinky agreed to meet and discuss some very important details concerning the future of the 50/50 Crew down in Florida.

"Speechless, this assassin bitch could be the fine broad I bagged down in South Beach my brother. The *chica* had the potential to be a top-notch bitch. Even on the Bonnie tip because she showed loyalty and fearlessness in her eyes." Chinky shook his head wishing he had more than his intuition. But hell, his gut feeling was strong, and couldn't ignore it.

"You sure?" asked Speechless.

"You know I got a good ass memory Speechless, and the way I call it, I be dead-ass accurate with my shit!" said Chinky.

"You think that's the same bitch huh Chinky?" Asked Speechless with the sternest and serious face he could muster. "This the same hoe you had big plans for once we moved the families down to Florida. Correct, Bro?" Speechless asked again.

"Yeah, my brother. That's what I am saying to you man. It sounds like the same bitch to me. And I am rarely wrong. That broad has to go in a nasty fucking way you hear me, Bro? I will handle this shit personally Speechless and track this bitch down along with this fucking weasel Baby Hatchet. Let U.M. and Twin deal with Baby Hatchet. I will take care of Ms. Cuba."

"Make it happen Chinky. Get that shit done so we can make these necessary moves. Take the jet, grab a mil out of the crew safe just in case you have to be gone for more than six months. But get this motherfucker Chinky, and take Dolly with you." And just like that Speechless ended the discussion and walked away setting the plan in motion.

NINETEEN
DOLLY

CHINKY

C hinky packed his shit immediately left Newark. Accompanying him on this mission was his twenty-year-old apprentice, Dolly. One of the finest, sexiest, curvaceous women Chinky had ever seen and he'd seem plenty. This young bitch was super-gorgeous, and the crush she had on Chinky since she was thirteen spawned a connection to him that turned into becoming his student and private assassin. She was a part-time freak and the most loyal companion he'd ever come in contact with besides his brothers in the 50/50 Crew.

Dolly was dedicated to this nigga for life, and he made sure that she had all the finer things life had to offer, from education to fashion, to cars and jewelry. Dolly was from the North Newark section of Jersey and ever since she was in the seventh grade, she would fantasize about being with the big-time drug dealer from around the way named Chinky even though he was six years older than she was. At nineteen Chinky, and his partner Pretty Boy were running most of North Newark that was not controlled by the Italians, and ran a pretty lucrative weed and crack cocaine business.

When Dolly turned seventeen and was a senior in high school, she'd blossomed in all the right places and began to attract attention, drawing all types of dudes at all ages.

Throughout the years, rumors had always popped up about this guy or that one was her dude because he did her homework or carried her books for her. One day, when she was leaving school a group of youngsters had approached her then formed a circle around her so they could torment and ridicule her for being conceited and antisocial. As one or two hooligans would jump in her face, someone else would come up from behind and pinch her or squeeze her ass until she was red in the face with anger.

"Hey! What the hell are you doing?" Yelled Dolly. Don't touch my butt! Don't touch me lame motherfuckers! Just because I don't talk to your dirty asses!" she went on.

"Fuck you bitch!" yelled someone.

"You ain't all that anyway hoe! Get the fuck out of here!" The shortest one yelled. Then out of nowhere, someone slapped her across the ass so hard you could hear the contact of his hand after he'd smacked her.

"You fucking bastard!" Tears of anger and embarrassment ran down her pretty cheeks, and she could taste the salt in her tears as she turned around and slapped the shit out of the closest one to her.

"What the fuck? Bitch! You slapped the wrong motherfucker!" He held the cheek that stung, and you could see anger burning in his eyes. "I didn't fucking touch you!"

"All of you are together! Take that shit up with your homeboy!" Dolly was angry and they'd all feel her wrath. "Don't none of y'all better fucking touch me again!" She eyed them all meaning every word she said.

All of a sudden, a white and chrome Alfa Romeo Milano pulled up with matching rims and clean as shit. Chinky rolled down the window looking past Diablo in the passengers' seat of the car and out to the ruckus. The crowd froze as he abruptly jumped out, Diablo right behind him, and walked over in their direction. Dolly could only see her knight in shining armor and had blocked out everything and everyone else.

"You motherfuckers got a problem with my Shorty?" Chinky flicked open a wooden handle 007 buck knife in a quick motion.

"Who the fuck are you suppo—" but the young punk's words were cut short when Diablo cracked him in the back of his head with a baseball bat made out of aluminum. The kid crashed to the ground.

"Oh shit!" Another hood screamed as he watched another one of his friends go down from a stab wound. Chinky had poked him a few times because he was the one with all the mouth.

"We don't want any probl—" but he never finished his sentence, as he too was knocked out with the baseball bat by Diablo.

Dolly screamed when somebody's blood splashed on her face, and Chinky flipped the fuck out thinking that she had gotten injured in the melee. He began to stab and slice any motherfucker that wasn't running or already knocked the fuck out by Diablo and his bat until his white sweat suit was burgundy with numerous blood stains. It was only then when no one seemed to be a threat anymore, did Chinky stop attacking, close the knife, and passed it to Diablo who jumped in the backseat while Chinky escorted Dolly over to his car.

"Are you alright sweetheart? Are you hurt or cut any place, baby girl?" Asked Chinky.

"No, no. I am okay now. Thanks to you. Thank you for your help. I don't know what they were going to do to me. They were mean as hell for no fucking reason," she said, getting angry as she thought about the incident! Tears of anger began to run down her cheeks and chin. Chinky put his arm around her shoulder and pulled her close to him as they walked to the car to comfort her.

"Don't you worry about none of that shit baby girl. I got you now. You are with Chinky and don't nobody fuck with me or my people. You understand me, sweetheart?"

"Yeah Papi, I understand you. And I ain't no punk bitch neither, just so you know that shit. There ain't nothing soft about this bitch right here!" she repeated.

"Baby, as long as I am your protector and your man, I don't ever want to hear you call yourself a bitch again in life. You hear me?" Chinky said to her sternly. "You are too gorgeous and have way too much potential for that dumb shit. Find a better word that describes you. ok?"

"Alright baby. It won't happen again, but you know what I mean."

"Good then." Chinky turned toward Diablo to introduce him. "This is my enforcer, Diablo. What is your name angel?" asked Chinky.

"My name is Dalia, but everyone calls me Dolly because it is easier to say," she said with an innocent smile on her face. "It's nice to meet you Diablo. And what is your name, my handsome knight in shining armor?" she asked Chinky.

"My name is Carlos, but the town knows me as Chinky, because of my eyes," he said looking in her direction and smiling. "My mom is from Korea, and my dad met her overseas fighting in combat. So, you can say that I am 50/50." He said. She smiled at that and reached for his hand as he drove to one of his many plush apartments to wash, change clothes, and relax a little after rescuing Dolly. He didn't even ask if she had to be home or not. He just drove the car she was his now. After that first encounter, Chinky had admitted to Dolly that he had his eyes on her since she was just a sophomore at fifteen years old, but he would not dare speak or approach her until she was a little older.

"What if you waited that long for me and I had a boyfriend or was married or something Papi? What would you have done?" She smirked.

"Then I would have gotten rid of him baby. Either it would have been my way or get found on the side of the highway!" Chinky laughed.

"You are one crazy motherfucker Carlos," Dolly laughed right along with him as they relaxed in bed and got familiar.

Over the months and years, they were almost always together. Chinky taught her everything about the game. Everything. He taught her how to shoot a gun, how to use a blade correctly without cutting herself, how to read people, and know when they are lying to her. He also showed her how to produce, package, and sell cocaine and weed. When it came to dealing with certain people, whenever Diablo was too intimidating or aggressive, Chinky would use Dolly because she was beautiful, deadly, and had much more finesse than any male killer he had known other than himself.

He taught her how to play nice, be seductive, alluring, and how to be stern and take no shit from no one! She was always dressed in the best designer fashions, smoked the best exotic marijuana, and dined at the best eateries from Essex County to New York City. He kept her long naturally beautiful hair done up every week, and her hands and toes boasted the latest designs: Gucci, Prada, Burberry. You name it, she wore it. She rarely had to wait in salons, and she went to the spa once a week for a full body massage.

Every big-time drug dealer in Newark or East Orange wanted her and tried their hardest to win her over, but she only had eyes and emotions for Chinky. This half-Oriental, half-Puerto Rican motherfucker was just so gangster to her and very well-respected everywhere they went. He introduced her to his closest partners and brothers, and she was received as family. Together they had taken the lives of the opposition and taken over territories, from Newark to Jersey City to Maplewood. They had weed spots everywhere you turned because they supplied seventy-five percent of smoke to three major cities in Essex County: East Orange, Irvington, and Newark.

TWENTY
MAKE IT HAPPEN

S peechless gathered the 50/50 Crew together, and let everyone that was considered a partner, know about Chinky's assignment down in Miami. At the huge mahogany round table, he told Gorilla, Pretty Boy, and Shorty Slice what the deal was and which direction the Crew was headed after the annihilation of Baby Hatchet and Ms. Cuba.

"Wow. That nigga was planning on doing big things with shorty down in South Beach," Gorilla said. "But that's our brother and one cold-blooded motherfucker so we already know the outcome of that mission. Chinky is going to make it happen," he continued.

"Yeah. That is one brother that plays no games at all. Him or Dolly, and I know if another bitch is involved, then she is right there with him and ready as ever," said Shorty Slice.

"He knows what he's doing and if anybody can get to that bitch, it is Chinky. Those damn slanted eyes always get him over with the ladies," said Pretty Boy smiling. "Chinky was built for this shit, just as we all are my brothers, 50/50 Crew is no fucking joke.

"He will handle business without question, that we are sure of my brothers, but if Baby Hatchet forms another Butcher Boys down in Florida, we are going to have a lot to deal with my friends," Speechless took a sip from his glass before reclining back looking at his brothers.

Together they spent hours planning, talking, smoking, and sipping on cognac. The time had come for them to move on and branch out into other states, other turfs, and be prepared to do whatever it took to succeed, as the 50/50 Crew always had.

After the meeting, Speechless went to see his main lady Patricia, and enjoy the other side of life. The side that was serene and drama-free.

"Hi sexy," chimed Patricia when she saw him enter the condo they shared.

"Hey, there gorgeous. How is my favorite police officer doing today?" Speechless scooped her up in his big strong arms and kissed her neck.

"I'm doing fine Daddy. I miss you so much," she moaned, kissing on his face and lips as he cupped her juicy soft ass and slowly moved to her mouth, nose, and forehead.

Clothes started coming and it wasn't long before they were completely naked and consuming one another passionately. Their harmonious rhythm felt like they became one complete body. Climax after climax, he brought her to heights of ecstasy proving to her why he is unquestionably the king in her life. He pleasured her in every way she would allow, and she consumed him in a complete act to end their erotic episode of lovemaking.

"Baby? When are we, going to get away from New Jersey, and put all of this behind us?" Patricia snuggled herself in his chest and arms. "We have more than plenty. And shit is getting worse and worse every single day out here, baby. When are we really going to pick up and just go?" She was adamant.

"Please be patient with that baby girl. There is so much going on right now with the businesses and this expansion into other states."

"I know that you have a whole lot going on, but when are we going to travel the world more and do us? Do more things Speech?" Her body stiffened and Speech could feel her getting riled up. "When are you going to slow the hell down and let someone else run your enterprise while we travel the world? Aren't you tired of New Jersey and the fucking states? I worry about you more than I do my damn self!"

"First of all, we travel and see more shit than rich folks. We been everywhere and anywhere you ever wanted to go. So don't give me that shit! Furthermore, I am never going to trust anyone to run my shit but me and my family. That's it!" He sat up trying to contain his agitation. "Don't be coming at me all differently and sideways now love, because you know what it is that I fucking do. And you know where my loyalty lies" he continued. "One day, we will all be done and retired, and old and shit. But that shit is a long way from now! Until then, we turn millions into billions and buy up as much of this county as we fucking can, while we can," he added resolutely.

"Yeah but—" she started, but was interrupted.

"Yeah, but nothing!" he barked as she stood up. "I don't want to hear any fucking doubts or questions, or none of that shit again Patricia. You hear me? I am who I am. Me and everyone around me are very, very successful!"

She looked at him with indescribable resentment and surprise, and she could not believe the words that were coming out of his mouth. As long as she had known him, he had never spoken to her disrespectfully or rudely in any way!

She did not know this man that was in her presence at the moment. She could not comprehend that they had just made love and yet, here she was feeling hatred towards the man she loves, mere moments after that intimate encounter. She knew that there was something he was keeping from her and that there was much more to him than the properties and the businesses he owned. Her intuition warned her that he did more than the contract killings for the mafia and that whatever he truly did for a living, he had been doing for a long time. She was dumbfounded.

"Are we going out to eat, or do you want me to cook something for you Daddy?" she asked calmly hoping to ease the tension.

"I feel like staying in tonight. Don't really feel like being out right now." He walked toward the Jacuzzi not turning back. "Cook whatever you like Patricia. I will eat later after I wake up. I need some well-deserved rest and alone time."

PRETTY BOY

On the other side of Newark, near Hawthorne Avenue and Bergen Street, Pretty Boy and Gorilla sat in a tented-up S600 Mercedes coupe. The triple–black sports coupe was barely visible under the huge tree and hidden away from the streetlights. The strip was thriving with activity and the usual hustlers, drug addicts, and street supervisors were ever-present.

The two 50/50 Crew leaders schemed and waited patiently for Big Lip Will to show up on the set. Big Lip Will was the leader of a small clique of paper chasers that got money down the hill named The Floss Family. They ran the areas between Bergen St. and Muhammad Ali Avenue, and the Avenues of eighteenth and Clinton. Although he made hundreds of thousands of dollars a month running the Double-F, Big Lip Will owed the 50/50 Crew a half mil and his ass had been ducking them for the last week. He'd avoided phone calls and the visits from the bosses of the 50/50 Crew. He got spooked when two of his Floss Family members had to be made an example of so that Big Lip Will got the message clearly. His connect was not playing any games either: They found the two young hustlers shot 5 times each. Three shots to the torso and two to the head), with a $100 bill stuffed into their mouths, according to the Chief Medical Examiner of Essex County.

Now, Big Lip Will was in and out of the area, and on and of the block periodically. But this trap they set for him was near where his children's mother lived, and he could barely stay away from her pussy all day long. It was just a matter of time before he wanted to get his dick wet.

"Listen 'Rilla," said Pretty Boy. "We don't kill this motherfucker until we get all or most of the money owed to us. You follow me, bro? I know that you hate this big lip motherfucker, because his first cousin was responsible for the kidnapping of Jamaica, but we have to stay focused and get this shit done. This pussy owes us half a million!" Pretty Boy was all hyped up.

"Nigga. Who the fuck are you fooling with? With your trigger-happy ass. The one we have to worry about shooting big lips is you motherfucker!" Gorilla cracked up. "As soon as he tries to flex his little jail weight up in your face and tries to talk tough, you are going to shoot him dead in his fucking face no questions. So cut the bullshit and don't give me that speech right there," he added.

"Yeah, yeah, yeah. Whatever Rilla! I just know he better have that fucking money when he shows the fuck up!" Pretty Boy scowled.

They decided to jet to White Castle on Elizabeth Avenue real quick while waiting on this nervous ass pussy Big Lip Will to show his cowardly face. They were only grabbing some milkshakes, so it shouldn't take that long to get in and out of there.

As they were coming through the drive-thru, Gorilla spotted the girl that Big Lip Will had children with, driving his pearl-white Porche truck with the purple-tinted windows and purple neon lights underneath. Her window was rolled down halfway so he could clearly see her running her mouth to some other bitch in another Porche truck. An orange one with orange-mirror tints and sitting on twenty-four-inch orange & chrome rims. He could also see the silhouettes of several other people inside the truck with Big Lip Will's baby mother.

"Follow that bitch Pretty Boy!" ordered Gorilla.

"You know I'm on it, bro. Fuck them shakes. I am not going to lose this bitch!"

They followed the white Porche truck as it made four different stops around Newark picking up cash. All the areas were within the territory of Big Lip Will and his Double-F clique, and Pretty Boy and Gorilla were veteran hustlers, so they knew what time it was. Every time they got out of the truck, two or three shooters were getting out the back and collecting bags. Then they would throw the bags in the back of the truck and pull off. Eight duffel bags in all. All of the money belonging to the 50/50 Crew.

"We are taking these motherfuckers down right now Pretty Boy! We got this, Bro, as soon as they park, they shit!" Gorilla excitedly reached in the back of Pretty Boy's seat and grabbed one of the many sub-machine guns stashed back there. Chambering a round, he told Pretty Boy to ease to a two car-length distance from behind and to be ready when they pulled up on them.

"Get ready, bro," said Gorilla.

Big Lip Will sat comfortably in the passenger's seat of the Cayenne truck, right next to his bitch giving play-by-play instructions on what to do, and how to go about doing it. He wore a bullet-proof vest, as did his baby's mother, which made her feel gangster and officially like one of the Floss Family who boasted their success by wearing the most expensive clothes and the biggest jewelry while driving around in the most expensive cars.

They neared a big house in the middle of the block with a gate around it and came to a complete stop. The driver noticed the gunman just a couple of seconds too late and was shot in the back of the head as the entire entourage bailed and abandoned the truck.

Gorilla and Pretty Boy opened fire on anyone moving in that truck or trying to escape the vehicle. Repeatedly they fired, moving swiftly covering both sides of the vehicle with gunfire as enormous empty shells littered the ground. Gorilla lit up the front seat, finishing off Big Lip Will and his bitch who was stretched out, slumped with half of her body still in the truck and the other half hanging out of her door. Pretty Boy was going around giving headshots to everyone they had just taken out, as Gorilla moved swiftly to recover the money. Quickly he began transporting the bags of loot to the Mercedes trunk and backseat.

"C'mon Pretty Boy! Let's get the fuck out of here pronto! Them motherfuckers are dead. I know that you hear them motherfucking sirens coming in the distance. Hurry up and help me with this money!"

"Here I come now but we can't leave any of these clowns breathing. Fuck that!" Pretty Boy remarked put another shot in the head of someone already dead before he brought over the last two duffel bags. He jumped in behind the wheel and sped off up the hill.

"You know we are going to have to clean all this shit up soon, don't you? Now that Fat Lip is dead and gone." Pretty Boy steered the sleek luxury stealth towards Vailsburg. Eventually, all of them motherfuckers are done, and ain't shit they can do about it." Pretty Boy laughed aloud.

"Yeah. In a minute we have to come back through this area and lock this shit down too. After the smoke clears, get the rest of these fake fly faggots, just like we got their big-lip pussy-ass boss. Rest in pieces motherfucker!" yelled Gorilla, giving Pretty Boy a knuckles-to-knuckles dap.

TWENTY-ONE
DOLLY & CLYDE

CHINKY

C hinky and Dolly checked into a plush hotel near Ocean Drive first checking into a backup suite on a different floor that would hold their cash and weed and be used just in case of an emergency.

"Baby, it is so nice down here. Damn." Dolly looked around at all of the palm trees swaying in the breeze and the melee of Ocean Drive. "There is so much to see and do baby. I want us to live down here one day," she continued.

"Of course, baby doll. We can live down here one day. We can make that happen, but all in due time baby, okay. First thing's first though, we have business down here. Our assignment is the focus. Business first, then fun second. Remember?" he asked her. "We have straight business Dolly, so don't get caught up in all the bullshit and atmosphere down here understood?" he stressed.

"Yes, Baby. I got you, Daddy. I'm cool. I'm just happy to be with you and away from Newark again that's all. It's been a while since we got away anywhere." Dolly rubbed Chinky's arm affectionately.

"Alright then. First things first. Shower, smoke, then we can go shopping while I line up some wheels to get around in. Later on, we can hit the streets and the strip clubs," Chinky said.

"Sounds great to me but when are you going to stretch this pussy out, *Papi*?"

131

"In the shower, we are going to handle all of that freaky shit you like. You thirsty?" he asked her.

"Hell yeah," she smiled. "I can get my drink on," she replied stripping down and walking towards the walk-up shower smiling.

BABY HATCHET

On the other side of Miami, Baby Hatchet and Cynthia were out collecting and checking on their people. They had to lay low for a few weeks since they had murdered one of the twins at one of the local malls. Baby Hatchet had listened to Cynthia as she had broken down her plan to him to reverse the hunt. Stalk their stalkers, then strike when they least expected it. It was supposed to be all three of the 50/50 Crew hit men that died that day at the mall, but Ms. Cruz just couldn't resist the opportunity when she was approached by the twin Gritty.

She smiled at him when the split-second of recognition registered to twin then slit his throat without even blinking an eye. It was as if she just slapped him across his neck. She turned away from him as blood leaked everywhere.

Baby Hatchet was there the entire time as backup. He was disguised as an invalid in a wheelchair, some old clothes and blanket that covered him, but underneath the blanket resting on his lap, was a silenced 9mm pistol. He was supposed to follow them to the parking lot after they had done their shopping and ambush them, as he pretended to beg for loose change, but Cynthia's anxiousness set them back a little bit. That chance would have to wait. Baby Hatchet had just the thing for those two clowns. He knew just who to call for this special job.

Ms. Cruz and Baby Hatchet made their rounds, stopping at places you would least expect to be safe houses for money and drugs: loan offices, mortgage companies, and dry cleaners. You name it and they were paying people to stash money there. Although his entire crew had been slaughtered by the 50/50 Crew during the bloody war they had, Baby Hatchet still managed to survive and stay bubbling on top of his game. Hell, when they ran him out of New Jersey, they actually brought him closer to his connect! *Those 50/50 punks helped me out. and they don't even know it.*

He and Ms. Cruz hit it off right from the start when they met in the strip club. He was always blowing five or ten thousand dollars in the clubs on a good weekend, just to keep up with the professional sports figures and the other ballers in the area. Cynthia was there, shining and looking incredible as always, and ignoring every baller and paper chaser in the building that was up in her presence. She had style, class, and was drop-dead gorgeous.

She also seemed to pay the women more attention than the men up inside the joint, and Baby Hatchet being the observant motherfucker he was, did not miss that fact about her. They exchanged glances a few times that night and Baby Hatchet secured himself a V.I.P. booth near where Ms. Cuba was so that she could see him.

He ordered four bottles of Cristal champagne and sent for ten grand worth of single dollar bills to be delivered to his table. Once the money arrived, he signaled for the waitress to take a bottle of champagne and a glass over to Ms. Cuba, along with a small note.

Join me over here gorgeous. I want to see the most beautiful lady in here dance in front of me.

When she read the message and looked up at him, he was staring back and popping the money bands off the stacks one by one, and starting to stack the money all over his table. As she walked up to his table and put down her champagne, he examined her sexy body up close and personal, and he was very pleased by what he saw.

"Dance!" he ordered, pointing to the spot on the right side of his table. As soon as she put her designer bag down on the floor at her feet, she started grinding and gyrating to the beat of the song playing. Almost immediately Baby Hatchet started showering her with money. He had small stacks of ones all over his table, and each little pile was a hundred in singles. Pile after pile, stack after stack, he grabbed and made it thunderstorm on her, showering her with money until her feet were completely covered. He continued this, as song after song played or was mixed in by the house D.J., and just when she thought he was done because her entire bag was covered with money as well, he reached for more money and made it rain so much that other dancers started to become jealous of Cynthia and started complaining to the management and bouncers.

The bouncers let the dancers know that he could spend his money on any female he chose to, just as long as he kept on buying alcohol and throwing money around inside the club. The bouncers also told the dancers to step their game up then maybe they could see some attention like this Spanish bombshell was receiving.

By the time Baby Hatchet was finished throwing, fanning, and tossing money at Ms. Cuba, she had a pile of money in front of her. All eyes were on her and that monstrous mountain of singles. The bouncers and maintenance guys assisted Cynthia with all her cash, and put it in a big doubled-up brown paper bag, after straightening out the bills and placing it into stacks it was easy to store into the bag. She tipped each one of them for their help even though they declined when she offered. When she came over to Baby Hatchet, he stood up and offered his hand to her.

"What's up gorgeous? It's nice to meet you. I'm B.H."

"Cynthia," she said as she took his hand, "but you can call me special because that's how you just made me feel up here, Big Papa." She winked and smiled before she lifted her chin in question. "What's the B.H. stand for huh? Hope that it doesn't stand for bitch hater?"

"Nah baby, it stands for Bitch Hero!" snapped Baby Hatchet before he smiled to let her know that he was only joking around with her. "Just B.H. baby. Just B.H. Let's just keep it at that. Alright, lovely?"

They sat in the strip club for hours sipping champagne and taking up a storm, flirting, and talking shit to one another about how shit would go down between them when they left the spot. She followed him, in a white Lexus coupe convertible, and he drove a leased royal blue and silver Ferrari towards his hotel suite because he never went to his place on the first or second date.

They showered together, fucked like they were old high school sweethearts reunited, then they smoked some of the best purple Miami had to offer. Afterward, they fucked some more until late afternoon.

Since that night at the strip club, they were always around each other. She was the boss bitch he needed to complete his stable as he rebuilt the Butcher Boys under a new name, The Terribles. Baby Hatchet was the reckless gangster motherfucker she needed to hold her down and lead her in the right direction. She knew all about South Beach and Miami in its entirety, and he knew all about cocaine and how to bring it back from liquid to powder again.

They cliqued really well, got rid of many adversaries in their climb to the top, and made a lot of money together. He had other bitches down in Florida of course, but she was his bottom bitch, and he did what the fuck he wanted to do. Cynthia on the other hand had only stepped out on Baby Hatchet once after she caught him in bed with two bitches and didn't have the respect to invite her at least. She was infuriated with him and had stopped dealing with him for two weeks. She moved out temporarily, and it was during that time when she met encountered this half Korean/half European gangster who was on vacation from New Jersey.

She will never, ever forget that special dude. Baby Hatchet, on the other hand, she thought, was thorough and all that, well-connected, and everything, he was still just average looking and shorter than most guys she preferred to deal with. She always passed on the shorter dudes that tried to talk to her regularly, because she at five foot ten felt superior and never submissive to men not even on her eye level. It was like she automatically didn't respect them. All but BH. She respected Baby Hatchet. She loved him, she thought. But truth be told, she had fallen in love with the slanted-eyed Don and would do anything to be with that dude again.

That dude did all the right things, in all the right places, at all the right times and he knew how to treat a lady. Although their time spent was short-lived, she could not ever forget him. When he went back home to Jersey, she reluctantly went back to Baby Hatchet and their life of grime. The two of them had their ups and downs as any couple did, but these two, however, had an understanding and mutual respect between two shady hustlers. They lived comfortably and didn't have any worries, except how to move all of the cocaine that BH's connect supplied him with. They had about ten drug houses and two drug strips on the East Side of Miami, and they collected a lot of money every day, fearing that their spots would be robbed or raided by greedy cops, so they didn't take any risks.

50/50 CREW

Meanwhile, Uzi Malik and Grimy were planning their revenge and retribution on Baby Hatchet and Ms. Cuba, and they had pinpointed a routine. "I'm telling you, Malik, they are at the strip club this weekend. Guaranteed Bro. We can take them out there and get the fuck out of this town for real!" Grimy was starting to hate Miami.

"You sure about that little bro? These two have to die for sure, and the sooner the better. They do be up in those tittie bars on the regular basis though huh?" asked Uzi Malik.

"Yeah, they do, and we have to check all of them too because they do be hopping from spot to spot sometimes spreading all that money around like they hit the lottery or some shit." Young Twin turned sideways and spit on the ground.

"Then those strip clubs are where we are this weekend! We are going to stick to them clubs like flies on shit. You hear me Grimy? Fuck that. They can't escape no more. No more second fucking chances for these two. We will be there until they show up. No more slip-ups!"

"Yeah, man. Those sons of a bitches killed Twin bro. They fucking die terribly," Grimy stared out in front of him, his anger seething. "They get the worse death."

BABY HATCHET

After making rounds and collecting money from the many trap houses they controlled, Baby Hatchet and Cynthia focused on how they would get rid of the hitmen from New Jersey that were after them once and for all.

Baby Hatchet contacted the Pocahontas Mamas chief captain Diamond and told her that it was urgent to meet with them, and that it was sweepstakes time, code for a high-paying contract and that they should not keep him waiting.

Cynthia and Baby Hatchet met up with Diamond, Gemma, Sapphire, and her twin sister Ruby at a late-night eatery off to the side of one of the main strip malls in South Beach where there were many people inside at that time of the day. The six of them requested a booth big enough to seat them comfortably and were seated by the hostess a few minutes later. Diamond spoke up first.

"What's good Baby H.? Long time no hear from. What's the deal? Lay it all out for us man. Shit. We've been bored as hell for a minute now out there," said Diamond.

"Yeah, man. Bitches have got to eat, and we got some big ass appetites," chimed in Sapphire.

"We are ready for whatever. You know that about us, so let's go!" said her sister Ruby.

"Okay. Alright. Hundred grand for each dead motherfucker. Half upfront and half when we read about these two in the local paper's obituary column. But this shit has to be done as soon as possible. Like this motherfucking weekend!" yelled Baby Hatchet. "They came down here from New Jersey. Those 50/50 Crew chumps that killed our people and destroyed our businesses up there, and now down here is where they will stay! We handled one of them bitches, but these two are all yours," he said placing three large manila envelopes on the table. The smallest of the three envelopes contained four pictures: two of Uzi Malik, and two photos of Grimy on different occasions. The other two envelopes contained fifty grand in each envelope. All one-hundred-dollar bills.

"I want to read about this shit on Monday!" Baby Hatchet said, leaning across the table towards the four gorgeous but deadly assassins.

"We got this Daddy-O," said Gemma giving Cynthia a stare back, because she was grilling the shit out of Gemma behind that remark.

"Daddy-O?" You better get your own Daddy hoe. This shorty here is spoken for bitch!" snapped Ms. Cuba.

"Hoe? Bitch! You better watch your fucking mouth cutie or get your jaw broken for talking shit quick, fast, and in a hurry!" Gemma responded loudly and had to be calmed down by her girls. "You better check your bitch before you need another one!" she continued her rant looking directly at Baby H.

As soon as she finished talking, Cynthia jumped up to lunge at her but was restrained by Baby Hatchet and grabbed up in a bear hug. Luckily for Ms. Cuba, because as she jumped up to get at Gemma so did the other Pocahontas Mamas and all with straight razors out ready to disfigure Cynthia beyond recognition.

"Chill the fuck out and sit down, Cynthia!" Baby Hatchett ordered her with his mouth to her ear. "All of you sit the hell down up in here like this. What's wrong with all of you bitches? And Gemma, you better watch your fucking mouth!" he voiced again.

"Or what?" They all said in unison. "You better watch your fucking mouth nigga. Who the fuck do you think you are talking to, huh?"

"Everybody cool off, relax, and sit the fuck down a minute," said Baby Hatchet, as he sat down in the booth and descended with Ms. Cuba in his arms still.

The Indian assassins reluctantly put away their scalpels and sat down resuming their regular posture, but all of them were staring at Cynthia as if she had two heads.

"Now take care of this shit and handle your business so that you can get the rest of your money. If done, before Monday I have will another envelope for you. Business is business. Get this shit done ladies," he concluded.

"Don't worry about shit. Them targets are as good as gone. Tee-shirt photographs you hear me?" Diamond smiled confidently as the Pocahontas Mamas stood up to leave. "Oh yeah. Make sure that you watch the news this weekend and stay tuned. Daddy-O," she smirked, and they walked away from a glaring Cynthia.

"Fuck those fucking Nav-a-hoes!" yelled an angry Cynthia. "I swear to you B.H., I am going to deal with them bitches one day soon! Believe that.

CHINKY

As they prepared to leave their hotel suite, Chinky and Dolly checked their weapons and cash stash to make sure that they had enough of both before they set out on their mission. After they were satisfied and ready to roll out, Chinky grabbed the Gucci tote from his luggage collection, and they took the elevator down from the eleventh floor to the lobby where they met with the valet, who delivered to them a brand-new Ferrari Modena convertible, courtesy of Exotik Rydes Unlimited.

They pulled away from the hotel focused and determined to get a lead on their intended targets so that they could get back home to Jersey and regular business. After securing the vehicle the day before, Chinky made sure that he stashed plenty of money and firepower. He loaded two semi-automatic handguns, and two sub-machine guns, along with plenty of ammunition and two grenades into the Gucci luggage that he would store in the car in the morning.

He and Dolly were already buzzed and never reckless they didn't need to ride around smoking in the whip and draw extra attention to themselves. Chinky liked to be laser-focused. They were headed in the direction of the strip clubs because Chinky knew that both Baby Hatchet and Ms. Cuba had addictions to the booby bars. He was going to see which ones were their regular spots. Chinky was smart as a motherfucker, and he knew how to maneuver in the streets. On any streets.

They drove through some main strips that were popping off on the same side of town and showed off a little at the corner when they caught a red light. All eyes were on them and that car. You could just tell by looking at them, they had money. Whoever they were, they were really stunting without trying, and the local haters took notice as well watching with envy from a distance.

Chinky and Dolly stopped to get something cold to drink at a convenience store with a drive-in parking lot, and when Dolly got out to get the drinks Chinky could see that they had been followed for a few blocks by someone in a silver Suburban with mirror-tinted windows. He had noticed a couple of traffic lights, that the same truck was still behind them but trying desperately to blend in with traffic. Chinky wasn't stupid. He quickly got out and retrieved the tote luggage from the trunk, then got back in the car, took out a Glock 40, and chambered a round. He put the pistol between his leg and the car door. He started to blow the horn to get Dolly's attention. Two quick toots, followed by two more quick ones meant potential trouble.

Dolly knew that was the distress code for emergency and in an instant, she came running out of the store with nothing in her hands and a scowl on her face, but she was trained to be ready for whatever came her way.

"Drive!" Chinky barked, now sitting in the passenger seat. Dolly put the super-fast car in motion and lurched forward with extreme power, swiftly navigating the powerful sports car through traffic and creating a way out of the crowded parking lot. She made it to the main street and the Ferrari took flight quickly reaching eighty miles per hour.

She drove the car like a pro and didn't stop for red lights either. She made the necessary right turns whenever Chinky told her to, but the Suburban was in view the whole time. Every turn, every small stretch, couldn't enough distance between them. Daylight, motorcycles, and traffic were all working against them.

Then Chinky saw it. Heading right towards them doing at high speed. "Lock it up! Lock it up, Dolly!" Chinky was yelling, navigating, and being Dolly's second pair of eyes. And she did not hesitate to go with how he led. Immediately pulling the emergency brake and spinning the Modena into a one hundred and eighty-degree turn, the car spun now facing the distant but quickly approaching Suburban.

Chinky half-stood and put one bended knee in his seat, placing his foot up against the back of the set for balance and unloaded one of the forty caliber pistols, all while the speeding black van he saw was getting closer to their rear, getting bigger and bigger in the mirror.

The ricochet of ammunition unloading filled the air around them like a symphony. He emptied the deadly handgun as the windshield shattered, the radiator and the people in the front seats of the Suburban caught the hail of powerful bullets.

"Now! Now! Now!" Chinky braced himself as Dolly swiftly made a sharp turn to avoid the Suburban from smashing into them. Instead, it drove head-on into the black Econoline van colliding and nearly making a mangled metal sandwich out of Dolly and Chinky inside the Ferrari.

The sound of the head-on collision was deafening, as glass and tires flew in every direction. Chinky put another clip into his .40 caliber pistol as he and Dolly fled the scene leaving behind bodies, lucky to still be alive. They quickly headed back to their hotel room to wind down and changeup.

TWENTY-TWO
TIME TO END THIS

CHINKY

Uzi Malik, Twin, Chinky, and Dolly all met up for dinner to discuss the demise of Ms. Cuba and Baby Hatchet. After the attempt on Chinky and Dolly, it was time to end this shit. Kill, then be out!

"I can't believe that these motherfuckers tried to jack y'all down this motherfucker and you two just got here. Damn! Enough of this bullshit. We got to kill these bastards twice just to make sure that none of them are coming back you dig. Make sure that they are fucking dead, dead!" Uzi Malik was getting tired of being the one hunted and Baby Hatchet always seeming to be one step ahead.

"Tell them about the strip clubs Malik. How that little weasel and that Spanish bitch of his be up in that building on the regular. Them motherfuckers treat every weekend like a fucking holiday!" Twin was anxious to give the intel. Vengeance for his brother was coursing throughout his body and every step closer to getting it, excited him.

"Which club Twin?" asked Chinky. "Narrow this list down for me because they die this weekend!" Chinky now had his own personal reasons for wanting those motherfuckers dead.

Twin pointed as he looked over the list. "Skin Unlimited. They call it S.U., Queen of Hearts, and Ballers and Broads a.k.a. B&B's. They are mostly up in B&B's though. The security in that spot is real tight and no one ever gets robbed in that joint, or coming out of there." Twin added letting them know what to expect.

"Ballers and Broads huh? It sounds like a whole lot of money up in that piece. And it sounds like that is where we all need to be this weekend. Let's end this shit!" said Chinky. "Dolly, tell them the plan, baby." Chinky sat back and gave her the floor.

"Okay, Daddy." Dolly leaned forward and broke it down for them giving every detail needed and answering their questions concisely. There was nothing that she and Chinky hadn't already thought of. They'd ran scenarios and thought of backup plans and counterattacks. After they went over what Dolly had explained to them, everyone was on the same page and knew what part they had to play. Uzi Malik and Grimy were to play the bar close, after retrieving their weapons from the strippers' locker room. Chinky would pay four dancers five grand apiece to sneak the guns inside and stash them somewhere in the locker room.

While Uzi Malik and Grimy were at the bar, Chinky would lure Cynthia away from Baby Hatchet, and while he did that Dolly would slide in and capture baby Hatchet's undivided attention. As soon as Uzi Malik and Twin saw Dolly make her move on Baby Hatchet, they were to make their move and make sure that he never left that strip club alive. Chinky would be escorting Cynthia out of the club amidst the chaos and confusion, and then she would surely die a horrible death. No doubt about that.

BABY HATCHET

Meanwhile, across the city, in an old laundry warehouse, Baby Hatchet and Ms. Cuba were briefing their new army of soldiers, The Terribles. At a ceremony this weekend, the top ten earners and shooters would receive a five-carat diamond-encrusted pinky ring along with a diamond Rolex to match. The ceremony was to take place at the Ballers

& Broads strip club this weekend and they would be celebrating the expansion of The Terribles into Tampa and Orlando, as well Miami.

For this event, Baby Hatchet and Cynthia spared no expense. They shelled out a hundred grand to rent out a quarter of the club, reserved for private use only. They also hired the manager of the club for twenty-five thousand dollars and told him to make sure that there were at least five firearms stashed around the club, and only Baby Hatchet and Ms. Cuba would know the location of the weapons. After it was all written down then passed the information on to Baby Hatchet and his female partner-in-crime.

SPEECHLESS

Speechless cruised around the streets of Newark in his customized Mercedes Benz truck thinking about a few serious issues that had to be straightened out before the 50/50 Crew could expand into other states. Especially Florida. The stealth-black GL truck was bullet-proof and bomb-proof, as well as fully-equipped like the rest of the automobiles in his collection, from the Ferrari to the Lexus, and everything in between. He had replaced his green Range Rover with the black Mercedes truck after Tammy died.

Memories of the car always brought back memories of her and how she was murdered. The loss was devastating to him, but like any 'official' gangster, he got over it quickly once he handled his business and avenged her death. The Butchers Boys got what they deserved. From the bottom of the food chain on up. All except for Baby Hatchet. How he had slipped through the cracks and got away boiled Speechless's blood. The memory of one loss always led to the memory of another.

Speechless smoked on a blunt of sour diesel as he drove from down the hill on his way to Vailsburg, and thought about his slain mentor Salvatore and those responsible for his death. He thought about Don Canelli and anticipated the day he would see the mob bosses' brains paint a wall. He was determined as ever with vindictive retribution. He also knew that Baby Hatchet and his bitch would die soon as well, because knowing Baby Hatchet, he was putting together a brand new team and trying to rebuild the Butcher Boys down in Florida. So long as Speechless was alive, the 50/50 Crew was not having that! He had to die soon. All of his enemies had to be dealt with, and swiftly because Speechless had big plans for the 50/50 Crew.

He drove down Grove Street, coming from South Orange Avenue, and made a right unto Eighteenth Avenue heading to Hooterville, so that he could talk to Shorty Slice. He was still recovering and taking it kind of easy since he had gotten wounded. Dealing with the murder of his wife wasn't making him heal any faster. He was wounded physically and emotionally. Although both hood niggas were not afraid of nothing and no one they were still very different. While Speechless could move on from grief quickly, Shorty's big heart needed more time.

Everyone was supportive of his recovery, but Chinky had missed his little bro and was upset that he was out of commission for a little while. While Speechless, Gorilla, and Pretty Boy were all pushing Shorty Slice to continue to rest up, Chinky wasn't. "Man, give that little nigga a razor and a baby nine and let him work. Let him be him!"

While Speechless and Gorilla would normally agree, on this one they didn't see eye to eye with Chinky. "Let the little warrior rest up. We can handle shit fine until he gets better." Speechless didn't voice it, but it wasn't the lack of physical strength that made him cautious. A man's mind is his greatest weapon and Shorty would get himself killed if his greatest weapon was off.

"Yeah, Chinky. Ease the fuck up on baby bro. I know you love him. Shit nigga. We all do. But that's the baby boy of our cabinet and just like me and you, he makes up the 50/50 Crew," said Gorilla.

"I know. I fucking know!" Chinky was agitated with the whole situation but one day he'd understand.

After reaching Shorty Slice's crib, punching in his combination to the security gate Shorty had gotten installed when he brought the property years ago, Speechless gained entry into the enormous driveway and connecting backyard. Inside the gates were four blue-nose pit bulls, weighing about 100 pounds each and fully trained. They all came charging at Speechless at full speed, but he didn't flinch because he knew these animals before they even knew themselves and at one time, he had held each of them in the palm of his hand one by one. Shorty Slice came out of the side door and Speechless barked a command at the dogs.

"Stop!" He commanded. They immediately stopped and wagged their tails happily, because of the familiar voice and smell of Speechless, and they waited for him to pat their heads. He acknowledged them all by name then he greeted his little brother with a quick hand slap followed by a brief bear hug. Shorty Slice hugged his big brother back with one arm because he was still a little sore from his injuries.

"What's up family?" asked Speechless, releasing Shorty Slice. How have you been my brother? How's the family?"

"Everything and everybody is good Speechless. Under the present circumstances. We all still miss Lil' Free a great deal. You already know," said Shorty Slice.

"Yeah. I know. That shit was crazy man. And although we can't bring her back, we made sure that a whole lot of motherfuckers died behind her death, Shorty. She can rest in peace."

"I miss you bro. I miss all of you motherfuckers. And the family does as well. Everyone misses their big uncles, but we are holding it together up here."

"I know little bro. Words can't begin to express how we all feel about you being out of work for a while, but hey, I guess you can say you needed the rest man, for real. That shit is not to be taken lightly at all. I almost lost my fucking mind when they killed my Tammy, but this is what we do and who we are Shorty Slice. The motherfuckin' 50/50 Crew. I understand completely. We are all mourning and trying to put the pieces back together. We are always here for you, my brother.

Anytime that you need us, and I already know that the shit is mutual. That goes without saying. The 50/50 Crew will be forever.

"You know you're absolutely right Speechless. It's time to get even more of what's due to us!" Shorty Slice nodded. "Come inside and get something to eat. It's been a long ass time since you've been over to the house just to chill."

Shorty Slice had his house decked out from top to bottom, and with all of the additions and renovations, the house had tripled in value, but he would never sell it because he and Lil' Free had picked this property when she was pregnant with their first child.

He and Speechless had both suffered tremendous losses, losing a loved one to the violence they were permanently a part of. That was the life they had chosen for themselves. But still, they would move on, because since they were teens, this was who they were.

They shot a few games of pool, both of them being exceptional billiards players and certified hustlers in the halls back in the day. They smoked sour diesel while the live-in maid prepared a small dinner.

As they ate and talked about the plans that were in motion, Speechless updated him on everything that was going on with the family. and the family's enemies and the 50/50 crew in Miami.

"So, Chinky and Dolly went down there? Plus, Uzi Malik and Twin are still down there too? Damn. That shit is going to be like the Fourth of July down there soon. That bitch Dolly don't play no games!" Shorty Slice was a fan and loved her skills and tenacity.

"Yeah. They are all on the case now, and we should be hearing some news about our foes first thing next week. That will be the last town that this motherfucker tries to monopolize. His ass dies this weekend!" Speechless felt his blood rush but tamed it.

The next Speechless left his little brothers' house the next day and went home to shower and change. He had things to do today. Very important things. After getting dressed and ready to roll out, he placed a call to Pretty Boy and told him to meet him at the car wash in East Orange on Central. Speechless then hopped into his yellow Ferrari

Modena and left his home in South Orange on his way to see Pretty Boy and talk business while their cars got detailed.

Pretty Boy was already there when Speechless pulled up, and he was showing off his new toy, a teal-green convertible Mercedes S550 sport coupe. Once out of their cars, they greeted one another with a quick five, followed by a brief two-armed hug.

"Damn Pretty Boy. That thing there is nice, bro. When did you pick this up, show-off? Speechless asked while looking down at the car that was clearly turning heads.

"This my baby here, bro, but she don't have anything on the yellow jack she parked next to. You always stopping traffic in that shit big bro," joked Pretty Boy. "I got her about 3 months ago. Just never drove her. Still got nine hundred and eighty-two on the motherfucking dash. She clean as fuck!"

They started walking up the hill towards Wendy's and talked about all the shit that was going on with the family, the families' enemies, and all of the shit that would be taking place soon. Inside Wendy's, they sat at a back booth facing the hospital and talked some more, Speechless sipped on water while Pretty Boy munched on two orders of fries and an orange soda.

"So, Dolly is down there with Chinky? And Uzi has young Twin with him still, and they haven't killed these motherfuckers yet, bro?"

"Yeah, they are all down there, and this shit will be finished real soon. We can't let this little punk Baby Hatchet get strong and become a boss down there. Start branching out and shit!" Every time Speechless thought about the repercussions of Baby Hatchet somehow succeeding it angered him.

"And with Big Lip Willie out of the way, we are going to be moving in downtown and down the hill with full force. We flooding that shit next week! There's, three to four million to be taken off of those streets every year. Easy. And with their boss dead, their connect is gone, so we become that to that area. They have no choice but to fall in line." concluded Pretty Boy.

"Indeed. We stand to make a substantial profit when we take over that section, and of course, they will line the fuck up!" Speechless replied.

After they finished discussing business and other family things, the two of them headed back towards the auto detailer to pick up their rides and promised to meet up later on in the evening to possibly take the ladies out somewhere.

Speechless knew that when he parted ways with Pretty Boy, he wasn't going to be meeting up for dinner or anything else later on that night. He had other plans. For the past two weeks, he had tailed Don Canelli, and no matter where he and his security detail would go, Speechless was there. When the Don went to visit his mistress, Speechless was there. At the theater, he was there. Whenever he traveled to his favorite restaurant in Bloomfield; Speechless was there too.

There was nowhere for the Don to hide without Speechless getting to him, except maybe fleeing the country. After almost being discovered during dinner one night, Speechless was forced to kill two of the Dons' six bodyguards when they spotted him suspiciously eyeing the Don from across the dining hall. He had on shades and a small afro wig with a hat attached to it as a disguise the night he had followed the Don to the restaurant, and he paid a female to be his fake dinner date.

But when she got up and went to the bathroom, they spotted Speechless hawking the Don, staring in their direction intensely. They got up immediately and started after him. Two of them bolted towards him while the other headed towards the female bathroom. He left with no other choice because he could not risk getting caught and tortured with sodium barbital before they eventually killed him violently.

So, before they could get too close, he bolted from the booth, not giving them a chance to see his face, and fled through the kitchen and out the backdoor, towards the alley. With two goons on his heels, he could hear their footsteps and breathing behind him as he hopped the first fence. By the time he hopped the second one, they were very close to him. Too close. Then in a blur, with speed unaware to the Italians, he stopped running and attacked the two pursuers with deadly intent. The first one, he chopped him across the throat with enough force to break a two-by-four, instantly crushing his larynx completely, killing him within a few minutes. After the sickening crack sound, the big linebacker-sized goon went down hard and fast. The underestimation no doubt cost him his life.

When he realized that his partner was not only down, but dead, the other bodyguard reached for his pistol, but he was too late. Speechless had lined him up with an elbow to the jaw, followed up with a spinning left elbow to the side of the head. Once he fell, Speechless was all over him and broke his neck easily. He fled the scene unharmed, and it was later released by the news that three bodies were found around the immediate area of the restaurant by a little kid taking the trash out that night. Two Italian males, ages twenty-eight and twenty-nine, and an African American woman, twenty-four years of age were found dead in the back alley a few yards from the restaurant. It was also said that the female was brutally beaten and apparently tortured.

Don Canelli was infuriated about the attempt on his life and the deaths of two members of his security detail. He reached out to any and everyone who could possibly find out anything about this stalker. He wanted answers and information about this intrusion into his world. He was still cautious after the death of Frank Imperioletti and his security, but he refused to remain in hiding or seclusion. He was stubborn. And powerful. He was the Don, head of the Canelli Crime Family and he felt beyond approach and untouchable for many years.

Everyone close to him advised him to lay low in Sicily, back home, while all the smoke cleared and dust settled in New Jersey, but the Don was stubborn and reluctant to leave. After countless warnings, pleas, and assurances, the unyielding Don finally agreed to go. He would be gone for at least a year while his army annihilated all of their potential enemies in New Jersey and New York.

One of the main reasons why he agreed to the temporary change was that his mistress of many years, the late Frank Imperiolettis' wife had agreed to accompany the family as they fled. She needed a break from all the stress and mental anguish she was suffering since her husband's death. She needed an escape and was seizing the opportunity now. All she really cared about was that the Don was safe, to love and pleasure her. They were leaving the country immediately after arrangements were made with the pilots and the private jet. But the Don wasn't leaving until all business dealings were passed on to the acting underboss Vincenzo Venettillo, that should take no time and they would be gone in two days.

TWENTY-THREE
ALL SCORES SETTLED

CHINKY

The weather down in Miami was blazing hot all day and sticky hot all night. Uzi Malik and Twin were getting ready to go to Ballers & Broads early so that they would only be remembered by witnesses as the guys who bought a lot of drinks and bottles. The ones who threw a lot of money around that night. They also wanted to be the only ones in the strip club that night sitting with weapons on them. They kept their attire basic and non-descript but still fly enough to not draw suspicion for all the money they'd be spending.

Inside the truck they had rented, they loaded two shotguns, two Mac-10 submachine guns, four 9mm handguns, and two grenades just in case of an emergency. They were ready. Uzi Malik knew that this accomplishment would propel him to the upper echelon in the ranks of the 50/50 Crew, and young Twin knew that he would probably become a lieutenant after this hit was completed, especially being that he lost his brother on this mission.

They had their orders, and the instructions were clear. Grab a seat at the bar and splurge on bottles and dancers until they saw the signal. They rode in the red Yukon Denali, listening to Redman and mentally hyping themselves up and preparing themselves for the important job in front of them.

Earlier in the day, around noon, Chinky gave Cynthia a phone call and at his assumption, she was very surprised and excited to hear from him.

"Hey, sexy ma. How have you been down here in all this nice weather? You been behaving yourself, right?" asked Chinky.

"Hi, sweets. I have been good. Getting this paper and living life to the fullest. Are you down here for business or pleasure baby? And are you trying to get inside me or what Daddy?" Cynthia asked him boldly.

"Yes. Yes. Hell Yeah. You already know I am planning on seeing your sexy ass tonight. I am down here on business and pleasure baby doll." Chinky didn't have to try. He was smooth without effort.

"Well tonight I have something really important to take care of, but I guess you and I could link up there then slide off somewhere. It's an all-night event, so we can disappear for a little while where you can make that disappear inside this box." Ms. Cuba laughed flirtatiously as she said it, but she meant every word.

"What's this important event sweetheart? I should be V.I.P. Up in that joint beautiful. Get me on that list! Can you make that happen for me, baby? Chinky asked.

"It's a private party, thrown by me and my partner in honor of our team and our success. I have seen and done a lot since the last time I heard you in my ear handsome. I am doing bigger things with my company now." Cynthia spoke confidently and impressed with herself.

"I see. I hear. So where are we linking up at love? And do I need to bring Roscoe with me?" asked Chinky.

"Nah. No need for you to bring your hot-headed friend that likes to start trouble," she said smiling. "You can save the fireworks for the Fourth of July ceremonies. Tonight, we drink unlimited champagne, smoke the best grade weed around, and spend this money well by having lots of fun," she added.

"So, give me the time and place and I will pick you up from wherever you are in the party and steal you for an hour or so. Cool?" And just like that, Chinky got exactly what he wanted.

Pocahontas Mamas

The Pocahontas Mamas were also ready to start rolling out to the strip club after they got turned up a bit first off, that Goose and E. All six of them that were going that night to B&B's, had on some type of catsuit or full-body one piece to show off their banging bodies and long natural hair. Three of them wore ponytails, while the other three wore their hair in long braids flowing down their backs. Diamonds and rubies were the jewelry they chose to rock that night, and the lights in the club would surely make sure that they stood out.

They only wore the best, most expensive shit too. None of that fake costume stuff. Their sponsors were rich and wealthy sugar daddies that basically splurged on their ladies with no limitations or restraints. From luxury cars to homes and high-priced jewelry, the Pocahontas Mamas wanted for nothing. The thrill was in the kill. These bitches were cold killers and they loved taking contracts. They were taken care of by doctors, lawyers, married millionaires, cops, and big-time hustlers abroad, but their main income came from setting niggas up. They took contracts from fifty grand up to a quarter of a million dollars. On occasion, even more. The higher the risk and amount of kills, the higher the price they charged.

Once they all were finished with their drinks, they checked and then double-checked their appearances in the full-length mirrors and vanities. Then Diamond, Ruby, Gemma, Topaz, Sapphire, and Emerald all left the exclusive beach house they had rented, leaving in separate cars as they always did on missions.

When the Pocahontas Mamas arrived at B&B's strip club, it was already jumping, and the enormous parking lot was filling up. It looked like an exotic car show inside of the parking lot, with all types of luxury automobiles flooding the property. They parked away from each other and got ready for business disguised as pleasure.

CHINKY

On the other side of town, Chinky and Dolly had just finished fucking and smoking two blunts were getting ready to roll out.

"Baby, we got to hurry up so that we don't have any issues with getting in the spot tonight," said Dolly.

"We are good baby girl. We are alright. Just make sure that you are strapped up good and tight when you suit up. These motherfuckers do not survive tonight you hear me?" Chinky said sternly.

"Yes, Daddy. I hear you and I am ready to get fucking busy. You already know this is what the fuck I do. One of the reasons I was put here in the first place!" Dolly strapped scalpels around her thighs and waist before putting on an all-black terrycloth sweatsuit by Donna Karan. Chinky had taught her that black, whether it was velour, suede, or terrycloth, always camouflaged the best and concealed almost anything small. Dolly could shoot a gun like a professional, but she loved to stab a motherfucker, male or female. Who they were didn't even matter to her. Ever since Chinky rescued her at the high school that day, she was hooked on him, and she had put that blade work in on numerous occasions for him.

She had the weapons on her legs under spandex biker shorts that almost reached her knees, and the weapons on her waist were tucked under a body supporter. She was ready.

Chinky put his hair back into a ponytail and slipped on a New Jersey Devils fitted hat. He and Dolly would arrive in separate rentals, so as not to cause suspicion. After the incident with the Suburban and the van, they were being extra cautious and had their getaway plan down to a science. As long as everything went smoothly, they would be in New Jersey within forty-two hours after the hit.

DOLLY

When Chinky and Dolly pulled into the parking lot of Ballers & Broads, they were really surprised at how huge the venue was and how large the parking lot was. It looked like a big car dealership with the club adjacent to it. It was the largest strip club they had ever seen. Chinky and Dolly had no problems getting in at all. He waved a hundred-dollar bill at door security and was in without a pat frisk. Dolly, who was three people behind Chinky, did the same and made it in without a search.

Inside was gigantic. Decked out everywhere in red and white, and there were mirrors everywhere to highlight the ambiance and the interior of the strip club. Immediately, Chinky headed towards one of the bars once he spotted Uzi Malik and Twin sitting there posted up. Dolly spread out and started walking the club. Unless you were from North Newark or knew her from high school, you had never seen Dolly before because Chinky kept her under wraps. All eyes were on her in the B&B club, and she couldn't help but switch her ass even harder as she walked.

She ignored all the whistles and catcalls and walked to the other bar across the club from where her team was waiting and ordered a bottle of Dom P. along with one glass. After getting her champagne and pouring a glass for herself, she continued to walk the club slowly and sip her bubbly so that she could use the act of drinking as camouflage for scanning the crowd.

As she began walking around the perimeter of the strip club, she passed the V.I.P. private party section of the place that was sectioned off, and the secluded area was a big as a bowling alley. Then someone grabbed her arm. She turned around with a superficial grin on her face, to see a smiling Baby Hatchet iced-out and obviously drunk out of his mind.

"Excuse me, baby. Can I please have twenty seconds of your time gorgeous?" Baby Hatchet bit his bottom as he stared at her like he wanted to eat her where she stood. Dolly recognized him right away from the surveillance photos she had studied but she played along.

"Twenty seconds nigga. That's all you think you need? I will give you twenty seconds playboy. Go for it, but let my arm go love. I am not your property." Dolly sweetly but with enough bite that you knew she meant it.

"Yeah. That's right. Twenty seconds is all I need to introduce myself and invite you to my private party over there." Baby Hatchet pointed toward the curtain and the velvet ropes. "I'm B.H. by the way, " he said extending his hand to her. "Would you like to be a guest of mine sweetheart?" He stepped in closer and continued to press.

"You got a lot of attention for a sister you don't even know Big Head." Dolly laughed. "My name is Lola." She added.

"Bighead huh? Why I got to be all that Shawty? I ain't tripping or nothing baby. Just getting familiar with a very attractive lady that appears to be single. Walking around pouring her own champagne in a strip club. Am I violating you, Lola?" he asked.

"Big Head because whenever someone introduces themselves to me with initials, I draw up my own conclusion what those initials stand for. Feel me 'B.H.'?" Dolly winked and made eye contact with Chinky across the room as he made his way toward them. "What kind of party is it anyway?" she continued.

"A private celebration for my organization!" he announced proudly raising his arms up beside him like he was king of the world. Showboating on another level. "I'm gonna own this motherfucking town soon and you could be my Queen without a doubt baby. I mean Lola," he added.

Dolly stepped beyond the velvet rope as he unclipped the clamp latch and escorted her into his party. Behind the curtain, she estimated about seventy-five people in attendance.

Chinky, after stepping into the club, spotted his brothers immediately and gave her the signal separate. He walked past them and said, "Grip up!"

"Already hot," remarked Uzi Malik to a passing Chinky, letting him know they had already retrieved their guns from the stash and were ready. Chinky then walked ten stools away from Uzi Malik and Twin and ordered an orange juice and vodka with ice. He sat down and dialed Cynthia's number.

CHINKY

"I'm here baby. Sitting near one of the bars in the back of the club wearing all black, and a ponytail. You can't miss me." He spoke confidently, his swag vibing.

"O.k. sexy man. I am on my way. Give me a second baby, and I will be right there. You can't miss me in this yellow number I am rocking handsome," she flirted.

"Cool." Then he saw Dolly talking to someone, so he got the fuck up and started moving in that direction. He saw her looking at him, and by then he recognized Baby Hatchet talking to her, then they disappeared behind the velvet rope and curtain that shielded Baby Hatchet's party from the rest of Ballers and Broads patrons. He quickly headed to the bathroom to prepare.

Once he got inside of the bathroom, Chinky secured himself in the handicapped stall and he started placing a lot of toilet tissue on the floor for him to step on. He then, removed his boots one at a time, pulling the false heel and sole to the right and then backward, allowing the entire bottom to come off of the shoe revealing a stash compartment. Each sole held two ice pick blades and one snap-together handle. He expertly put the weapons together quickly, putting one ice pick in each pocket then he left the stall to wash his hands. He left the bathroom to meet up with Ms. Cuba.

He spotted Cynthia coming from behind the curtain and velvet rope, dressed in a bright-yellow halter top, matching yellow Manolo stiletto boots, and yellow and white denim booty shorts. She was still fine as a motherfucker, and he couldn't wait to get his dick in her mouth again. She could suck a raisin through a straw! They gave each other an embrace, followed behind him kissing her on the neck briefly, and then she escorted him to a private room. Once inside the room, she was pulling out his manhood before he had a chance to sit down, and sucking him royally. Like the professional she was.

DOLLY

As Dolly and Baby Hatchet walked by a crowded table of people, a waiter came up and delivered a note on a tray to Baby Hatchet. He read the note while they continued to walk around, then Dolly saw him pass the note off to a beautiful female that was relaxing with a bunch of other ladies, and they all looked alike. The bitch and her look-alikes then got up and left the private party to go into the main part of the club.

POCAHONTAS MAMAS

Gemma and her Pocahontas Mamas quickly scattered around the strip club retrieving hidden automatic handguns that were stashed in five different locations throughout the club.

Uzi Malik and Twin got side-tracked all of a sudden and distracted by four fine-ass bitches with banging bodies approaching the bar, walking directly towards them. At that same moment, two more superstar-status females sat right next to them at the bar. Uzi Malik was the one to notice that shit wasn't right when the women sat a little too close. As if they were professional pickpockets or something.

"What's up, ladies? What's good with you all up in here beautiful? You two dancing tonight or getting dances?" asked Uzi Malik as he fingered the pistol in his pocket and the one inside of his waistband.

"Nah, Daddy. We are here for the party!" spoke Gemma, as she reached from behind her back and brought up the powerful gun to Malik's chest and squeezed the trigger twice.

"You fucking bitch! Ah, shit!" said Uzi Malik as he grabbed his chest instinctively, and squeezed off four shots in her immediate direction from his own gun. Two of the women went down from the impact of the .40 caliber hand cannon.

Twin tried to spring into action, but he was caught off guard by the girl sitting next to him because he briefly froze up after seeing Uzi Malik get shot in the chest. The hesitation cost him his life. Diamond squeezed point-blank at the left side of Twins' head spraying the bar and Uzi Malik with Twins' brain fragments. Twin never even got a shot off. He was dead before his body hit the floor, gun still in hand. Then Uzi Malik started staggering forward blasting away at anything that seemed like a threat to him. Stray bullets flew everywhere as the remaining Pocahontas Mamas started shooting back at Uzi Malik, hitting people and dancers in their necks, shoulders, faces, and arms with roaming bullets. Innocent bystanders were dropping everywhere in the club.

CHINKY

Although Chinky could not hear the gunshots over the music and the chaos going on, as Ms. Cuba swallowed his load and was slowly taking her lips off of him, he was in mid-swing with the icepicks. Both weapons struck her in the sides of her head, then face, neck and chest. He was all over her body and face with deadly pokes. She was responsible for the death of Twin at the mall. She was instrumental in all of their future plans being at risk and in jeopardy, all because she was linked to their arch enemy, Baby Hatchet of the Butcher Boys.

Chinky thought about all of this as he delivered blow after deadly blow again and again until she was dead. Although he had put on gloves while she was sucking him off, he wasn't worried about any DNA because Chinky was the only 50/50 Crew member to never be arrested. Ever. He didn't even have a parking ticket his entire life, so he was in no criminal computer system or DNA databanks.

After making sure that she was dead, he left the private room to a melee of patrons running and falling all over the place, as he made his way in Dolly's direction. Then he saw Uzi Malik. He was wounded badly and shooting his way out of a mob of bitches that seemed to be all over him, and they had him surrounded. He was then met with a choice: save his woman and counterpart Dolly, or save his brother, and in that instant, he defined what true brotherhood means as he ran in Uzi Malik's direction. The black ensemble he wore helped to conceal him from the female killers' awareness as he advanced on the pack of females with deadly intent, stabbing anyone that wasn't conscious of his presence. Ruby and Diamond saw him stabbing one of their sisters to death and let him have it, squeezing their weapons in his direct area. He was hit in the chest, left shoulder, and the inner thigh near his scrotum. He was fucked up bad, with no bullet-proof vest of any kind.

Uzi Malik reached around his back, pulled out a Mac-10 submachine gun, and with mortal wounds to his chest and several slashes from scalpel attacks across his arms, shoulders, and back he started spraying the women left to right and right to left with bullets. The submachine gun rang out, cutting some of the Pocahontas Mamas in half and creating separation between them and a seriously wounded Chinky, who was on the floor bleeding badly. The deadly weapon just simply mowed down the women, and whoever got caught up in the crossfire.

Chinky, although he was hit three times, was a strong motherfucker, and was a workaholic in the gym with Speechless and Gorilla. Even with those wounds, he still had his eyesight. He could see the bodies of women dropping everywhere and a few patrons that were just innocent bystanders in the club trying to get away, dropping as well. He could see Uzi Malik stumbling towards him spraying the automatic compact Mac-10, and that's when he saw Twins' lifeless body. His eyes were wide open with surprise, and the wound on the left side of his head was even wider.

He saw the Glock 40 still inside Twins' hand. He crawled on his elbow and kicked and dragged his legs over to Twins' body, grabbed the fifteen-shot weapon, and began to stand up when he saw the bitch slashing Uzi Malik's throat. She had apparently gotten the drop on him and jumped on his back as he madly shot into the crowd in front of him. The scalpel opened his throat severely and he was on the verge of death, his only focus now was getting to his wounded brother and making sure he made it out of there safe. Maybe she jumped off the bar? However, she did it, she had gotten him good because he dropped his weapon and grabbed at his throat as he struggled to get to where Chinky was laying, only to get slashed across the back and stabbed repeatedly as he collapsed face-first to the bloody floor that was trashed with bodies, drinks, broken glass, and lots of blood.

Chinky was up on his feet now, and immediately he blasted the woman that killed Uzi Malik. He shot her up close and personal as she turned around surprised by him out of nowhere because she thought he was dead. Chinky shot her in the head and neck then shot her twice more in the head when she fell. With only eleven shots left, he pushed on to search for signs of Dolly. Limping and fighting the pain, he pushed forward and tried to avoid the oncoming frantic crowd that was rushing towards him, fleeing to get out of the strip club.

As soon as Baby Hatchet heard the gunshots and the loud screams, he forgot all about the lovely Lola sitting beside him and quickly retreated to his private room to get his strap! Dolly also stood up and as the people in the private party ran back and forth in panic in front of her, she made her move, rolling up her jacket and undergarment that hid the scalpels from plain view and held them in place. Removing two scalpels, she ran after Baby Hatchet only to be confronted by two of his gigantic personal bodyguards. They were huge men, each of them weighing nearly three hundred pounds. But they were just muscle, and they were unarmed up in the strip club. They were no match for a killer of Dolly's caliber.

She sliced with no mercy, slashing into their hands, stomachs, arms, and legs. Whatever she could touch on them when they tried to grab her, was instantly opened up, causing a floodgate of blood to flow. She hit the main arteries in their wrists, pelvis, and necks and before they knew it, they were bleeding to death.

She stepped around them and through the curtain to the private room quickly scanning the area in search of Baby Hatchett but didn't see him. Spotting an exit, she ran toward it. Chinky saw Baby Hatchett step out from behind a curtain and before he could call out to Dolly, Baby Hatchett shot her in the back of the head. She fell to the ground in a heap.

"You motherfucker!" Chinky screamed at Baby Hatchet as he dumped the rest of his clip at Baby Hatchet. He was out of ammunition but had hit Baby Hatchet in the shoulder and ass as he fled the private room letting off his own four shots at Chinky. One of the wild bullets hit Chinky, grazing his left wrist. Then, Baby Hatchet was gone, he had completely vanished from the scene. He was gone.

Chinky made it to his car barely conscious and grabbed his cell phone out of the glove compartment. He speed-dialed Speechless as quickly as he could and sped out of the parking lot before he passed out.

"Chinky?" asked Speechless. "Everything is everything?" he continued.

"Big bro, it's me. I'm down. And everybody is out. They got Dolly man. She gone. And them Indian bitches, they got Twin. And Uzi is gone bro. Went out like a garage…" Then the phone fell from Chinky's hand, as he lost consciousness.

"Hello. Hello! Chinky! Chinky! Hello! Pick up the motherfucking phone Bro!" Speechless screamed into the phone, but his calls fell on deaf ears as Chinky laid there in his car in an underground garage somewhere in Miami, bleeding to death.

Speechless placed an emergency call to Gorilla.

"Hello?" asked Gorilla. "Speak."

"It's me Rilla. They got our brother, man. Uzi Malik is dead. So is Dolly. And Twin too, " said Speechless his voice expressing concern and worry.

"What about slanted-eyes Speechless?" Gorilla asked. "Is Chink alright? Talk to me man!" Gorilla persisted.

"He is dying Rilla," Speechless said calmly. "We got to go get him now bro. Call the pilot and tell him to ready the jet. And bring your bag big fella. It's Chinky man. It's Chinky. And I think Baby Hatchet got away because he didn't mention anything about him," continued Speechless.

As Speechless got dressed, he thought about his brothers and what they had built together. He thought about what they were getting ready to go to Florida and do and the possibility that he might not make it back home. Then he stopped midway through packing his war bag when the phone rang. It was Gorilla.

"We leave in one hour Speechless. The pilot said that's the best he can do. I'm ready!"

"Alright. I will call my ace in the hole down in Miami and have him get to Chinky and get him to a doctor until we get there and bring him home. Don't worry Rilla, that half-breed is tough as fucking nails. He is one of us."

"Hello," answered Tito in his heavy accent.

"Family emergency," Speechless said. "I got a brother down there that needs help and a doctor ASAP, you hear me? His GPS on his phone tells me that he is about a mile southeast of the B&B strip club. Possibly in some kind of tunnel or covered place where he could hide his car. I got a million cash for you when I get there in about three hours, Tito. This is a favor brother," Speechless said emphatically.

"Consider it done. I just left my house."

That same night. in a quiet section of New Jersey's Northern region, Don Vito Canelli, his family, and his cohorts were preparing to leave for their secluded retreat to lay low for a year or two, before returning to the states again. Surely things would be very violent in his absence, but he would be responsible for that bloodshed and mayhem throughout the Northern part of the state. Newark, North Newark, East Orange, Bloomfield, Irvington, Caldwell, Jersey City, and Kearny would all be affected by the war to come.

Everyone was milling about and trying to get last-minute things to take along and taking care of personal needs. "Make sure that you brush your teeth children," said the Don. "As a matter of fact, why don't all of you brush your fucking teeth before you leave for this trip. We have all eaten hefty plates of pasta, seafood, and an abundance of garlic. So please, everyone please brush your teeth before you board the transporting vehicles, thank you. That's an order," stated the Don.

They had a caravan of five vehicles, all vans with smoke-tinted windows, going to the private airstrip. Two of them were for the Don, his family, the widow of Frank Imperioletti, and his cabinet and the other three vans contained security guards, weapons, and lots and lots of food and supplies. Thirty people in all were leaving in two separate private jets to the retreat in the Fiji Islands.

Don Vito walked toward his master bathroom to brush his teeth and grab his passport on the way back downstairs. He passed his wife, who was sitting on the bed just taking in the ambiance and décor of the house she was about to leave behind for God only knows how long.

"My love, make sure that there are plenty of cases of garlic and olive oil packed up before we leave alright sweetheart?" asked the Don of his wife, while he walked into the bathroom.

"Yes, Vito. I am taking care of it as soon as I get downstairs. How else am I supposed to cook dinner every night?" she said sarcastically. "Now hurry up because we have to go. The children and everyone is packed up and ready to leave as you have commanded. The extra vans are filled to capacity with food, clothes, and everything we will need. Now let's go Vito Canelli," said his wife.

Don Vito grabbed his electric toothbrush and put a generous amount of toothpaste on the toothbrush, then started brushing his teeth and thinking about the long flight they had ahead of them. As he rinsed to brush a second time, he started to think about his son sentenced to all of that jail time.

Those sons of bitches are going to pay for the shit they did to my Joey.

No one knew about the loophole in Joey's case that could win his appeal and possibly reverse the entire case. And the Don wasn't saying shit to anybody. Not even his worried wife. The only ones that knew besides the Don were the lawyer and Joey Jr., and as far as he was concerned, no one else needed to know a damn thing.

Don rinsed out his mouth again and washed his face. Afterward, he stood erect to look at his reflection in the mirror. He grabbed a hand towel and wiped his face off so that he could take in his appearance in the mirror, but something in the reflection froze him and pissed him off instantly.

It wasn't that favorite hand towel wasn't where it was normally placed. He chalked that up to the fact that they were temporarily moving, therefore someone clearly moved his towel. And his favorite pictures and slogans that he read every day while relieving himself were still hanging on the walls where they normally hung, so it wasn't that either. What made Don Vito Canelli, boss of the Canelli Crime Family angry, was the gloved hand that was sticking out of his shower gripping a silenced pistol. He closed his eyes. For the last time.

EPILOGUE

Tito Calversero was carrying out a promise. He was a man of integrity and morals and always kept his word. He and his two-man team of killers, Marko and Tony, searched the area for signs of Chinky or any abandoned exotic sports cars that were maybe left on the side of the road, or in a ditch. The immediate area near Ballers & Broads strip club was chaotic, and there were cops, ambulances, and fire trucks everywhere, as well as news reporters.

News vans and reporters scrambled and fought for room in search of an exclusive interview with any of the survivors or witnesses. Tito, Marko, and Tony passed through the area like tourists, but they had an arsenal onboard their Audi A7 sports sedan that could take out an entire precinct. They drove two blocks up the street from B&B's and ended up in front of Hermania's Parking Garage.

The structure was immense, almost an entire block long with six levels of parking, and an underground level for long-term parking. They paid the gate admission, and then they proceeded underground to look for Chinky. Tito was told, that if he was indeed holed up in a garage, that he would be located near the farthest back wall, where one could go no more. It was practice and protocol of a 50/50 Crew member in distress or trapped to follow that plan to avoid being apprehended at the hospital and risk being discovered or killed. He wasn't sure which vehicle Chinky was in but Speechless said that it would no doubt be a flashy ride. Tito placed an emergency call to Speechless.

"Yeah, " answered Speechless.

"It's me. We are here my brother, and we are very close I can feel it, but do you know what his car looks like? Or can you try his cellphone? There are lots of cars down here Speech?"

"Hold on Tito. Rilla, call his cell," Speechless asked. Chinky's cellphone started ringing in Gorillas' ear. "It's ringing Tito. Listen out for him. We should be arriving shortly." Speechless kept his voice calm and collected despite the worry for Chinky's life.

In the enclosed rear part of the bottom level inside the parking garage, the rap song How About Some Hardcore by M.O.P. could be heard blaring from a distance. Then it stopped. Then the song started again. They were drawn toward the Eastern corner of the garage as Gorilla kept calling back again, and again.

"I can hear him. I hear rap music playing somewhere close by Speech. We are getting out of the car now." The three goons got out of the Audi, then walked two cars down to a convertible Corvette, black with black interior.

"We got him Speech. I mean he's bad bro. Real bad. It's been too long for him with no help," said Tito sympathetically. He moved in closer to get a better look at Chinky. "There's so much fucking blood, bro. " Tito continued.

"Just check his fucking pulse for me Tito!" yelled Speechless into the phone losing his cool. "Is he alive?" Speechless asked. "Check his pulse!" he repeated.

"Hold on," said Tito, handing the cellphone to Marko. He checked Chinky's pulse, both wrists, and then his neck. They were both very faint. "He's alive! He will live if he has lived this long. We got him. Hurry up and get here! I'm taking him to my dad's old patcher. This motherfucker Chinky is strong as shit bro. Help me get him out of this car boys! Tony, get the door and clear the backseat of the A7. Hurry up Speech! He's fucked up bad, but he is alive!" shouted Tito.

"Thanks, Tito. Words are not enough bro. We will see you in an hour." Speechless slammed his phone down relieved then he looked to

Gorilla. "They got him Rilla. He's safe. Lock and fucking load!" Speechless commanded.

SW TCH H TTER

PART TWO

50/50 Crew:
'Til Death Do Us

A NOVEL BY
KARRIEM BILAL MUHAMMAD

ABOUT THE AUTHOR

Karriem Bilal Muhammad, is a Newark, New Jersey native whose Muslim background has kept him well–balanced and focused. He aspires to change the lives of those around him by being successful and encouraging others to reach their dreams.

He founded his own publishing company, Move The Chains Publishing, with a focus on urban fiction literature. His first novel *Switch Hitter*, the first in his series of four total works, was published in 2021 in collaboration with Urban House Publishing.

Karriem is on the road to being a notable name in Urban Fiction and Black Authored literature.

Made in United States
North Haven, CT
05 May 2022

18924216R10105